Clayton's River Adventure:
Mobile to Destin

—— by ——
Linda M. Penn & Frank J. Feger
Illustrated by Melissa Quinio

Acknowledgements

Thanks to God for allowing us the time, enthusiasm, ideas, and words to complete this project.

Thanks to Judy, Frank's wife, and Gilbert, Linda's husband, for their support.

Thanks to Melissa Quinio for bringing Clayton, family, and friends to life in this book.

Thanks to Misty Baker, Editor and Layout Designer, for her technical expertise.

Thanks to the people we interviewed for giving us their time and relaying so much first-hand knowledge:

DeAnne and Scott Shellinbarger – Mobile to Navarre Beach, Intracoastal Waterway
Julia Warfel – sailboating
Janice Watanabe – Dauphin Island
Donna Federspiel – Pensacola, Perdido Key, and Blue Angels team
Paul Thomas – Navy submarines
Gilbert Penn – Navy battleships
Sharon Dillon – Destin

TO ALL THE CHILDREN WHO WILL BE READING THIS BOOK – ENJOY!

Sincerely,
Frank and Linda

DISCLAIMER:

Table of Contents

—— Chapter 1 ——
Hello, Granny Rose!

"Hello, *Granny Rose!*" Clayton called as he, Mom, Grampy, Clayton's friend, Austin, Grampy's friend, Mr. Scott, and faithful dog, Daisy, exited Mr. Scott's car. They saw Grampy's houseboat docked down the pier of the Spanish Fort Marina in Mobile, Alabama.

"Thank you, Mr. Scott, for picking us up from the airport this morning," Austin said.

"Yes, Mr. Scott," agreed Clayton. "Let's go see that mansion on the water." Clayton pointed ahead to the houseboat.

Clayton, Austin, and Daisy walked faster along the wharf, wanting to sprint to the boat, but knowing the marina's rule was no running on the pier.

"Come on, everyone!" Austin said as he turned around and waved for the group to speed up their walking. "There she is! She looks so lonely. We haven't seen her since last summer."

"Go ahead, we'll be there shortly," Grampy answered, out of breath. He had that admiring smile on his face as he saw his houseboat after its long journey from Paducah, Kentucky, guided by Mr. Jim and Mrs. Samantha.

"Those youngsters certainly are excited to participate in another water adventure," Mom said, with a beaming face. "Well, really, I am thrilled also."

"Electrifying!" declared Mr. Scott. "Look at the boys, reaching out from the pier to try to touch the *Granny Rose* and there's Daisy jumping around and barking excitedly at the boat."

"Bet she remembers our adventures on the Ohio and Kentucky Rivers last summer," added Mom.

After Grampy led the group onboard, Clayton and Austin proceeded to reverently stroke the steering wheel of the *Granny Rose*.

"Oh, wow, that plane ride this morning from Louisville to Mobile was exhilarating," announced

Clayton, "but...well, nothing compares to being right HERE on the bridge of the *Granny Rose* again."

"I second that," Austin responded as he perused the Intracoastal Waterway maps that Grampy had removed from his backpack.

"You know what, boys?" Mom said. "I really miss our other deckhands – your friend, Camryn, from the Kentucky River adventure and Clayton's cousin, Sydney, from the Ohio River adventure."

"Me too," Clayton agreed. "Sure hope they will make it to Destin this Fall Break. Their last emails said they weren't sure if their families could make the trip."

Mom and Grampy then exchanged those silly-looking grins that they had shown in the past when surprises were on the horizon but unknown to the boys.

"Clayton," Austin said quietly as he nodded toward Mom and Grampy, "something's up."

"Oh yeah, I saw those crazy grins," Clayton whispered back. "I'm just glad that we know for sure my Dad is flying down when we get to Destin, and it will be fun to have your parents there too."

"Sure thing!" Austin laughed. "More adventures on the way."

"Before we get underway on the water adventure on the houseboat," Mr. Scott said, "I was thinking today on my way to the airport about some places you might be interested to see around Mobile."

"Okay, I'm on it," Clayton answered. "During the plane ride, I researched on the iPad about the Mobile area. Is everyone ready for all my newly attained knowledge?"

After a hearty laugh from the group, Grampy answered, "Super, Clayton, hold on to those thoughts until we get back in Mr. Scott's car to tour Mobile. We need to check out the *Granny Rose* to make sure she is Intracoastal Waterway-ready for our trip from here to Destin. Mr. Jim and Mrs. Samantha told me everything was fine as they piloted the *Granny Rose* down the Tombigbee Waterway from Paducah to Mobile and docked here, but it's probably a good idea to check the boat over before we depart tomorrow. Mr. Jim and Mrs. Samantha are so anxious to see you when we arrive in Destin. We will catch up with them in a couple of days."

"Okay, Captain Grampy," Austin saluted. "I'll check the ropes and buoys."

"I'll check the kitchen area," Mom offered. "I'll make a list of supplies we need."

"I'll test our safety equipment," Clayton responded. "Flashlights, bullhorns and flashers."

"Great cooperation as usual from you deckhands," Grampy complimented. "I'll be in charge of checking the engine, the gas tank and the water tank."

After a thorough examination of the *Granny Rose*, Grampy announced the houseboat was safe and ready for the water.

"We are off for a quick lunch and then a tour of the USS Alabama and the USS Drum at the Battleship

Memorial Park," Mr. Scott said, "but sorry, Clayton, Daisy will not be permitted on board those ships.

"Daisy will be fine in her kennel while we are gone," Clayton said as he prepared Daisy's food and water and then opened the kennel door for her to enter.

"Off we go, then," Mr. Scott said, pointing the way to his car. "I'm a Navy veteran, so I never pass up the opportunity to tour the ships."

"Alright!" Clayton answered as the group headed down the wharf to the car.

—— **Chapter 2** ——
Flags Over Mobile

"The Mobile area was first inhabited by the Native Americans as far back as 10,000 years ago," Clayton began. "They were known as 'shellmound people' because they ate so much shellfish. There were as many as 18 shell mounds, one being 50 feet high. The mounds still exist today and are a National Historic Landmark."

"Glad you told us about that. We will get to see shell mounds tomorrow on Dauphin Island," Mr. Scott said."

"Mobile has had flags from five countries fly over the region. The Spanish began exploring the area in the early 1500's, and Hernando deSoto, a Spaniard, encountered the Muscogee Native American tribe led by Chief Tuscaloosa at Maubila. This is where the city of Mobile got its name. The Spanish remained in control until the late 1600's, when French troops established Mobile as the capital of French Louisiana."

"Weren't the French the first to celebrate Mardi Gras in Mobile?" asked Grampy.

"Yes," answered Mr. Scott. "The Mardi Gras is celebrated in cities all over the U.S. now. One of the many museums in Mobile is the Mardi Gras Carnival Museum. It displays the history of the carnival and has replicas of costumes and floats that have been in previous Mardi Gras parades."

"Mardi Gras is French for Fat Tuesday," Mom said. "It's the celebration for the day before Lent which is the season of fasting for many Christians. It lasts about six weeks, ending on Easter Sunday."

"Yes, I always give up chocolate candy for Lent," Austin boasted.

"Me too," Clayton nodded. "Mom, every year I ask you and Dad if I can give up vegetables."

"And...every year, I have to explain you need to give up something you really like," Mom laughed.

"But doesn't that make Easter morning much more special?" Mr. Scott asked.

"Oh, yeah, I dive into a big chocolate bunny!" grinned Austin, licking his lips.

"Since Christians believe Jesus was sacrificed for us, our giving up something special during Lent represents our honoring Him with our sacrifice," Grampy explained.

"Fat Tuesday, huh?" exclaimed Clayton. "Hey, Austin, next year, we need to eat chocolate, chocolate, and more chocolate candy the day before Lent begins."

"Awesome idea, buddy," Austin agreed as he and Clayton held their arms way out to simulate having rotund bellies.

"Sounds like fun, but...I remember getting super sick when I was a little girl because I gorged myself with all kinds of candy on Fat Tuesday," said Mom with a frown.

"Okay, way too much talk about food!" Clayton suggested. "I need to finish up letting you in on my Mobile knowledge."

"Go for it, Clayton," Mr. Scott suggested. "We're almost to the Burger Barn for lunch."

"The British arrived in the late 1700's when Mobile became an English colony. They declared the Mobile area as the healthiest place to live because of the clear fresh water and air. A famous British naturalist, William Bartram, was commissioned by the King of England to study the area. His journals about plants, birds and the waterways were published in 1791."

"That sounds similar to what John James Audubon did," remarked Austin. "I remember learning about Audubon during our last river adventure on the Ohio River."

"Oh, yes, we saw those wonderful detailed, realistic paintings of birds at the Audubon State Park in Henderson, Kentucky," Grampy recalled.

"Cool! Okay, are you listening?" Clayton asked. "Just a little more to tell about this SUPER historic city."

"The next change of command in the region came when Spanish troops captured Mobile during the American Revolutionary War and they built the Old Spanish Fort to guard the harbor. The area thrived in the 1800's and Mobile became part of Alabama, the 22nd state of the United States in 1819. Steamboats carried passengers, cotton, pottery, farm products, turpentine, and lumber, but then the Civil War began, with Alabama joining the Confederacy. Union soldiers overpowered Confederate forces at the Old Spanish Fort and nearby Ft. Blakely in 1865. Mobile, Alabama was once again part of the United States."

"So proud of you, Clayton," Mom smiled. "You were right. Mobile is really a super historic city."

"Yes, buddy, I know you are a history buff," Austin said, giving Clayton two thumbs up. "Can't wait to share my research about Dauphin Island, but I will probably have to review my notes before tomorrow morning, just to keep up with you, Clayton."

Mr. Scott pulled into the Burger Barn parking lot and everyone quickly exited the car, heading to the front door.

"Alright," Clayton hailed. "I could use a big burger, but after all that talking about Mobile, I mostly need a GIANT gulp of water."

—— **Chapter 3** ——
Tight Squeezes

After everyone in Grampy's group enjoyed their burgers at Burger Barn, they quickly got into Mr. Scott's car and he drove into the parking lot at Battleship Park.

As they headed up the gangplank to tour the USS Alabama, Clayton exclaimed,

"That ship is a monster, and look at the size of the guns."

Grampy opened the brochure given to the group at the Admissions Desk. "The USS Alabama has the title of 'Heroine of the Pacific' due to her duties in World War II. She carried approximately 2500 men and she had 12 decks. In 1943, she headed to the North Atlantic and then to the South Pacific, where she earned nine Battle Stars. Her adventures ended when she led the American Navy fleet into Tokyo Bay in 1945 at the end of the war. She was due to be scrapped by the U.S. in 1962 because battleships had become obsolete in the naval defense of America. However, a group of Mobilians led the way for her to become a tourist attraction in Mobile Bay. The Battleship Memorial Park opened in 1965, and it also has the USS Drum, along with planes, helicopters, tanks, a Korean War memorial, and even a dog statue."

"Dog statue?" questioned Clayton. "I don't want to miss seeing that."

"Yes, dedicated to Alabama's War Dogs, the four-legged soldiers who died while serving in the U.S. armed forces," Grampy said.

"This ship seems like a small city," Mom observed as the group began their tour of the 'monster.'

"Mr. Scott, were you on a ship like this when you were in the Navy?" Austin asked.

"Yes, my second assignment was on the USS Newport News, a battleship, stationed at Norfolk, Virginia. I had been on a destroyer, and when I first saw the battleship, I, too, called it a 'monster' because it was at least 20 times larger than my destroyer. My new ship had an Admiral onboard, so we had to keep everything spick and span because we never knew when a Congressional member or even the President might come aboard. After our boatswain's whistle blew at 6 a.m., we had to get some of our chores done before breakfast. One of our chores was to wash and mop the decks every morning, and we had to do it again in the evening."

"Oh, how tiring," Mom grimaced.

"Everyone of us sailors took turns at the daily chores," Mr. Scott responded. "Most of our Sundays were days off and we had movies and recreational activities in the evenings, but there were always about 30 men on guard duty at all times. We got mail delivery about 3 or 4 days a week and had hookup to TV when we were in port. A big plus was that I got to 'see the world,' at least parts of the world I never would have made it to on my own, and met lots of good buddies, so I enjoyed the Navy time."

"Even these tight squeezes?" Clayton laughed as the group made their way through the narrow hallways to view the sleeping quarters. "Oh, wow, I have slept in two person bunks, but, look, these are three person bunks!"

"We all got used to life on the ship after a few days," Mr. Scott smiled.

"Hey, Austin, you okay, buddy?" Clayton asked. "I remember your phobia about tight places."

"Well...I don't really like these close hallways and rooms, and I feel a little sick, but I'll be okay, I think..." Austin said with sweat running down his forehead.

"Take deep breaths, young man, focus on your watch. You can see that time is really passing. Keep telling yourself that anxious feeling you have will go away in just a little while," Mr. Scott suggested.

"Yes, sir, I got this," Austin responded with a determined look on his face.

"When I joined my first ship's company, everyone offered me saltine crackers for the nausea and seasickness. I ate a lot of crackers back then," laughed Mr. Scott.

After the tour of the lower bunks, Austin was then able to smile. "Life's good!" he professed, as he entered daylight and firmly placed his feet on the outdoor deck of the ship.

"Austin, are you ready for the USS Drum, a submarine?" Grampy asked.

"Yes, let's go for it! I'm conquering this claustrophobia," Austin proclaimed. "Hey Clayton, dude, how about your acrophobia? Are you going to look down at the water from the railing on this high deck?"

"Hey, man, yes, absolutely! I will crush that phobia," Clayton replied as the group walked to the railing. Clayton slowly...slowly approached the rail, shaking a little, breathing a little deeply, looking straight ahead. He gripped the railing tightly and gradually lowered his head.

"I made it!" Clayton shouted as he bent over the railing and peered at the ship's side and the water of Mobile Bay below.

"Fabulous, youngsters, proud of you," Mr. Scott said as he, Grampy and Mom high-fived both of the boys.

"Onward to more tight squeezes," Clayton said, pointing to the submarine docked just down the pier.

Grampy began reading from the brochure again. "The USS Drum was launched in May, 1941 and was the first Navy submarine to enter combat in World War II, cruising off the coast of Japan. She earned 13 Battle Stars and was enroute to her 14th patrol in the Pacific when the Japanese surrendered in 1945. The sub had a 76 millimeter deck gun, a 40 millimeter auto cannon, and a 20 millimeter cannon on its deck for protection from an aerial attack when the sub was above the water. She was 311 feet long and could proceed at a rate of 21 knots above the water and 9 knots below water. She could stay submerged for 48 hours. The USS Drum was decommissioned in 1946 and became a tourist attraction at Mobile Bay in Battleship Memorial Park alongside the USS Alabama.

The submarine carried up to 75 seamen and 8 officers. It could descend to a depth of 300 feet. A pet dog named 'Stateside' lived on the sub with the men."

"Wow, how exciting!" Clayton said. "Dogs were important to the war effort."

"Yes," Grampy replied. "I have a friend, Pete, who has done duty on a Navy sub, and he talked about the men taking care of a stray dog that adopted the men and the ship as its home. Pete said he loved having this 'little comfort of home' with him on his long stints of duty. As a matter of fact, he even owns his own submarine now. Of course, it's nothing like the updated and high-tech subs in today's Navy. Subs and aircraft carriers have become the most important vessels for our country's water system defense."

"I want to hear more later about this sub that your friend owns, after we tour this ship," Austin said, as the group walked down the gangplank to board the USS Drum.

"Look at the periscope sticking out from the top of the deck," Austin said. "Amazing how subs are able to draw the periscope up and down to see enemy ships. Talk about major POWER!"

"Hey, if you totally conquer that claustrophobia, you might change your mind from being in the Army to becoming a Navy man someday," Clayton laughed. "Who knows? Maybe me too!"

The group then climbed down the steep steps to view the sub interior. "Tight squeezes again," Mr. Scott smiled as he drew himself in to be as narrow as possible.

"Okay, ready to locate those enemy subs! UP PERISCOPE!" Clayton commanded as he saw the gigantic machinery in the control area.

"Enemy ship sighted, Captain Clayton!" Austin answered. "Target locked in, ready to shoot torpedo!"

"Fire one, fire two!" Clayton ordered.

"Target hit!" Austin shouted.

"Okay, Captain Clayton and Co-Captain Austin, let's move on to the eating and sleeping quarters," Grampy suggested.

"Except for the hallways being a little tighter, and the kitchen area being a lot smaller, the sleeping quarters are almost as close as the battleship," Mom observed. "I really don't think I could live like this for days and days. I love the *Granny Rose*, but even that seems a little cramped now and then."

"It's just a lot of friend and family quality time in close quarters!" Grampy smiled, as the group ascended the stairs to the gangplank.

As they departed the USS Drum, Clayton, Austin and Mom seemed to be shaking their heads as if wondering if they could live on a Navy ship for long periods of time.

"I have a much deeper appreciation for Navy personnel now," said Mom.

"Yes, and the more I think about it," Clayton pondered, "I believe I would really like to 'see the world' onboard a Navy ship, DOWN PERISCOPE!"

"Let's head back to the car, you deckhands," Grampy said, motioning the way down the pier.

"Thanks, Mr. Scott, for touring with us today," Clayton said, as the group climbed into Mr. Scott's car to head back to the Spanish Fort Marina and the *Granny Rose.* "I'm going to hustle down the pier super-quick-like, when we get back – gotta check on Daisy!"

"You're welcome, Clayton, and I really had fun today, brings back good thoughts," Mr. Scott replied. "I know you are really going to enjoy tomorrow at Dauphin Island. You'll be able to see it all with Daisy, as long as she is on a leash."

"Yes!" exclaimed Austin. "By the way, Grampy, can we hear more about your friend and his own submarine?"

"My good buddy, Pete, retired from the Navy, moved to Destin, found a yellow submarine for sale, and decided to buy it."

"YELLOW SUBMARINE?" Clayton inquired. "Wasn't there a song about a yellow submarine?"

"Sure was," Grampy nodded, as he hummed the tune.

"Grampy, you mentioned Destin. Your friend lives there, like... NOW?" Clayton asked, his eyes getting huge.

"Are you hinting about something?" Mom asked.

"Well, Mom, you always seem to know what I'm thinking, so...sure would be fun to see a submarine, particularly a YELLOW one!"

—— **Chapter 4** ——
Dauphin Island Awaits

"Rise and shine, crew," Grampy shouted to the boys in their below deck bunks. "Time to get underway! Dauphin Island awaits!"

"Okay!" Clayton answered, as Daisy licked his face.

"Yes, we are on it, Grampy!" Austin called as he patted Daisy's head.

The boys dressed quickly in anticipation of another water adventure on the *Granny Rose*. Daisy could tell something was up and began jumping around.

"Come on, girl, let's go to the wee-wee mat and get your food and fresh water," Clayton said as the boys and Daisy climbed the stairs to the main deck.

"Good morning, fellows, oatmeal and bananas ready," Mom said.

"Great! Can't wait to get underway," Clayton said, giggling like it was Christmas morning, as he gulped down his breakfast.

"Can you believe it has been three months since our last water adventure, Grampy? But I still remember everything you taught me," Austin said, finishing his cereal. "Bumpers, buoys, life jackets, flashers, and on and on."

"And I remember how to read the gauges in the wheelhouse," Clayton assured Grampy.

"Super, you deckhands!" Grampy said, giving a thumbs up. "Gas tanks filled? CHECK! Water tanks filled? CHECK!"

"So glad we restocked our supplies at the marina store last night," Mom said. "CHECK! Cabinet hatches secured? CHECK!"

"Daisy, what have you checked off on our preparation list? Oh, yes, you are going to be on guard for floating debris at the look-out post on the top deck with me?" Clayton patted Daisy, and together they made their way up the ladder. Ready for our watch, girl? CHECK!"

When the departure checklist was completed, Grampy cranked over the engine. Everyone broke out in a spontaneous shout of excitement and pumped their fists, as Grampy put the gear in reverse and backed out of the marina space.

"That engine's purring is the best music I've heard in three months!" Austin declared.

After Grampy successfully piloted the *Granny Rose* out into the Mobile Bay traveling channel, Austin continued to look over Grampy's shoulder at the wheelhouse studying all the gauges.

"Grampy, do we have a map of Mobile Bay? So we know where the channel is and any underwater hazards like sandbars or unusual depth changes?" Austin asked.

"No, I do not have a map of the bay but we will keep between the red and green buoys, and stay to the right side of the channel. That is the general nautical safety guideline. Anyone who is moving at a greater speed than us can then pass on our left."

"A water highway," Mom said. "Basically the same guidelines on the rivers that you learned about on the last adventure apply here in the bay."

"We'll keep our eye on the depth gauge to make sure we don't run into a sandbar," Grampy said. "And we can all keep our eyes focused to spy for any large floating debris."

"Do we need to call ahead for permission to dock at a marina like we did on the rivers?" Clayton shouted down from the top deck.

"Sure thing," Grampy advised. "Austin, will you use the marine radio on channel 13 to call the Dauphin Island Marina and ask for permission to dock for the day? Plus, we need to get permission to dock tonight at the Pirates Cove Marina at Orange Beach."

"I'm on it, Captain Grampy," Austin replied.

"Look out there, Daisy!" Clayton said. "Is that a periscope sticking out above the water?" Daisy began to bark and climbed into Clayton's lap.

"Uh, uh...Grampy, there is something out in the water port side, looks like a long antenna," Clayton shouted.

"Don't see a thing," Grampy answered as he looked port side. "Maybe the sun was making a shadow on the water."

"It's gone now," Clayton said as he hugged Daisy. "You okay now, girl?"

Daisy climbed down out of Clayton's lap, her barking having subsided.

"Maybe it was the sun, maybe not...we saw something, didn't we, Daisy?"

Daisy barked loudly, affirming Clayton's words.

"We are assigned dock number 18, starboard side, for Dauphin Island, and dock number 11, starboard side, for tonight at Orange Beach," Austin reported.

"Fantastic, I'll write that down in my notes," Mom said.

"It's time, everyone!" Austin bellowed. "Clayton, buddy, on top deck, can you hear me?"

"Yes, loud and clear, what's up?"

"It's that time for me to impart my Dauphin Island knowledge to this group!"

"Yes, Austin, let's hear it!" Mom smiled proudly.

"Dauphin Island was first inhabited by Native American tribes, who enjoyed the fishing there and mounds were formed using shells from the numerous fish. Today, Shell Mound Park marks the place where the mounds were and it is a favorite bird watching place. The island was then settled by the Spanish and then the French in the mid to late 1600's. The British then came and then Americans, just like the history of Mobile you told us about, Clayton. The island was named by King Louis 15th of France after one of his daughters. The island is a barrier island to Mobile, acting like a guardian to the large city. It is known as the 'Sunset Capital of Alabama' because of the fantastic views over the Gulf of Mexico.

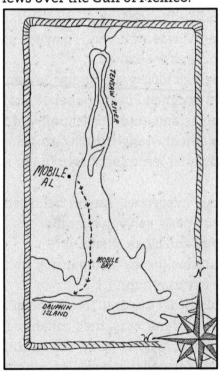

The island is 13 miles long, and only two miles wide. The early inhabitants brought over animals like pigs, cows, and goats from Europe and the animals were allowed to roam free. There is a famous spot on the island, called the Goat Trees, where the goats would climb into the trees. The island remained mostly rural until a three mile bridge from mainland Mobile to Dauphin Island was built, which opened in 1955. Some locals were not happy about the bridge because they wanted the island to remain rural. The bridge was destroyed by Hurricane Frederic in 1979, and eventually reopened in 1982, which is when commerce really began to boom on the island. Hotels, restaurants and other businesses thrived, although today many restrictions are still in place about any expansion on the island. There are four high-rise buildings, and lots of rental units available for visitors. The population is now about 1200. There is a ferryboat that serves one end of the island to Ft. Morgan on the mainland, and there are trolley stations spread around the island to transport visitors, avoiding traffic jams with so many cars and so few roads."

"Austin, good research!" Grampy acknowledged.

"Wow, sounds like we are in for a treat today," said Mom. "Let's settle in for the hour's trip to Dauphin Island and enjoy the beautiful surroundings."

After about 45 minutes of relaxed reading of his comic books and keeping a lookout for any hazards, Daisy's restlessness alerted Clayton. Next thing he knew, she was jumping in his lap and barking wildly.

"What is it, Daisy?" he said, trying to hug her tightly.

"There it is again," Clayton shouted. "That antenna, or periscope, or whatever it is, port side!" he called down to Grampy.

"Sorry, Clayton, I don't see anything unusual," Grampy answered.

"I'm coming up there, man," Austin told Clayton.

"Okay, Austin, buddy, I saw it," Clayton said, as Daisy climbed down from his lap and stopped barking, and Austin took a seat on the top deck.

"Hey, I am NOT joking! There was something out there sticking straight up." Clayton kept shaking his head as he took the iPad and typed in 'submarines' on the search line.

—— **Chapter 5** ——
Daisy and the Goat Trees

"Hey, deckhands," Grampy called up to the boys on the top deck. "We are nearing the island, so we need to prepare the *Granny Rose* for docking soon."

"Alright, Captain Grampy, Sir, we are on our way down to gather the buoys and ropes," Clayton bellowed.

Mom, Clayton and Austin completed the preparation for pulling into the boat slip at the Dauphin Island Marina while Grampy carefully turned the huge steering wheel at the houseboat's main deck and ever-so-perfectly parked at the number 18 dock.

"Engine turned off, ropes secured to the pier, hook-up to the water and wastewater tanks completed, electricity plugged in," Grampy acknowledged. "CHECK!"

"Okay, explorers, away we go," Mom said. "Grab those water bottles and make sure your journals are in your backpacks. Daisy, are you ready?"

Daisy was jumping around, and licking Clayton's hand, knowing something exciting was happening. Clayton secured Daisy's leash, the group exited the houseboat, and after a short walk to the trolley stop on LeMoyne Drive, the group was ready for a day of adventuring.

"Good morning, I'm Martha," nodded the trolley driver to Grampy's group as they boarded the trolley. "Where are you off to today on Dauphin Island?"

"Hello, Martha, I'm Grampy, and this is my daughter. Here is my grandson and his friend, and we are planning to stop at the Goat Trees and then walk to the Indian Mound Park."

"Nice...I'll let you off at the Cadillac Square stop, but I'll give you a little word of caution, especially since you have that cute dog with you."

"Miss Martha, this is Daisy," said Clayton. "Is there a problem?"

"Oh, no, just a little friendly story for you about those Goat Trees," Miss Martha replied. "Do you know why they are called that?"

"I researched about the island and read a long time ago the goats would climb in the trees," Austin said.

"Never heard before today that goats could climb in trees," Mom laughed.

"Let me tell you the goat story," Miss Martha offered, as she sat back in the driver's seat, turned over the trolley engine, and made her way out onto the thoroughfare.

The group was all ears, sitting on the edge of their seats, in anticipation of a special story.

"Dauphin Island had remained pretty much the same as when the Native American tribes settled here. When the Europeans came over, they brought their cattle, pigs, and goats with them. Everybody worked together, fishing being the main way to survive, and the animals wandered freely, including alligators, who frequented the island and the shore. There were few snakes, however, for the early inhabitants to deal with, because they were eaten by the hogs."

"Glad to hear that!" Mom beamed.

"Oh, yeah!" Miss Martha agreed. "In the 1950's, when construction began on the bridge to the mainland, one morning a construction crew heard loud scrambling noises in the large oaks close to where they were working. Guess what? When they searched, they found goats climbing down out of the trees! Further investigations found that in the evenings, the goats would line up under the trees, then pull themselves up, lie on their stomachs, and wrap their legs around the branches to sleep. Then, in the morning, the goats would all climb down, only to return to the trees for their nightly climb."

"Wow, why didn't they just sleep on the ground?" Austin asked.

"Well, the construction workers had been wondering why there were so many goats on the island with all the alligators looking for food," Miss Martha said. "Turns out the goats were just protecting themselves from getting snapped up by the alligators at night."

As the boys opened and closed their arms like hungry alligators, Miss Martha continued to weave her account of the history of the goats and other livestock. "The government officials knew that with the new bridge to Mobile, there was no way the roaming animals could co-exist safely with the numerous amount of visitors the bridge traffic would bring. So, the livestock animals were rounded up and transported by barge to Mobile. That law is in effect today also - no horses, goats, or any livestock allowed."

"Yes, certainly had to be done with hotels, restaurants, shops, and fishing charter boats thriving on the island," Grampy acknowledged.

"Miss Martha, you mentioned you had a word of caution for us today?" asked Clayton. "So... is Daisy in some kind of danger?"

"Just be careful, and hold tight to her leash when you get close to those trees," Miss Martha said. "There are stories about people seeing a lady ghost wandering the grounds. Supposedly she was a jilted bride and keeps looking for her bridegroom."

"Oh...Daisy is used to dealing with ghosts!" Clayton exclaimed. "Remember, Grampy, the ghost who supposedly took my shoes at Buttermilk Falls?"

As the group all looked intently at Grampy, he bent his head down, shaking it side to side. "Yes, Miss Martha, I confessed to a little trick on my grandson, about a ghost who took people's shoes, back in Brandenburg, Kentucky."

"Uh, oh!" Miss Martha shook her finger at Grampy as she pulled into the trolley stop at Cadillac Square. "Have a wonderful time today on the island. I'll be driving the trolley until 5:00 o'clock, so I might catch up with you later on my rounds."

"Thanks for the exciting information, and I'll be sure to hold onto Daisy tightly,"

Clayton said, as the group exited the trolley and looked over the map of Dauphin Island.

"This way!" pointed Clayton.

As everyone was leisurely walking to the Goat Trees, all of a sudden Daisy began barking and pulling on her leash.

"Come on, Daisy, it's okay." Clayton reached down to pet her, but she continued to bark. "I know we are getting close to the Goat Trees, so...are you sensing something weird?"

Daisy continued to bark and look to the sign on the trail giving information about the Goat Trees. Clayton walked carefully among the trees, holding onto Daisy's leash.

"Did you see that?" Austin yelled, pointing to a group of trees. "A lady with real long hair wearing a white dress, over there, by that huge oak tree with its limbs reaching out and almost touching the ground."

Daisy jumped and then ran around in circles, getting her leash twisted around Clayton's ankles.

"Daisy must have seen her too," Clayton replied, "but, sorry, Austin, dude, I didn't see a thing. Was it the bride ghost?"

"Well... she was all dressed in white, couldn't make out a face though. I'm ready...to...get out of here!" Austin stammered.

"Me too!" Clayton agreed. "Come on, Daisy, let's find a calm place and regroup."

"Wait! I see something – it's in that big oak tree!" Grampy called. "Look over there!"

"Is it the bride ghost?" Austin yelled.

"No, it's a goat!" Grampy replied.

"Well, I don't see anything in that tree," Clayton responded, shaking his head.

"Me either," Austin said, looking at Grampy with a quizzical stare.

"Okay, Grampy, is this another one of your made-up ghost stories?" Clayton rolled his eyes.

"Enough talk about ghosts. Let's head over to see the shell mounds," Mom suggested.

"I'm ready to get away from these Goat Trees!" Clayton pointed in the direction of the Indian Mound Shell Park as he looked at the island map.

Clayton made sure Daisy's leash was untangled. "Come on, Daisy, let's find that peaceful place so we can all recover from our shaking."

—— **Chapter 6** ——
Stingrays & Alligators

"The mounds were really high but too bad we can't see stacks of shells at the Shell Mound Park," Clayton commented as the group walked from the park to the trolley stop at Cadillac Square.

"The shells have all fallen apart over time," Mom added, "but all the greenery on the top and sides of the mounds was so beautiful, and those graceful, gorgeous herons flying right over us!"

"Yes, this brochure mentions the shell area is a great place on the island to bird-watch," Grampy said.

Upon reaching the trolley stop at Cadillac Square, Grampy read the schedule, "Next trolley will be here in 20 minutes. This is the center of town, so, let's walk around for a little while before we take the trolley to the Estuarium."

"Grampy, I wonder who General Gorgas is. This street is named General Gorgas Drive," Austin observed.

"Hmm, I'm not sure. Look, there is General Anderson Place," Grampy said.

"Clayton, do you have the iPad?" Mom asked. "Let's search those names."

"I'm on it," Clayton answered as he typed in General Gorgas and then General Anderson. "Here we go...Josiah Gorgas, an American Civil War general. General Robert Anderson was also a general in the American Civil War."

"Very interesting," commented Grampy as he perused the island map. "Apparently all the streets off the General Gorgas Drive are named for generals. After General Anderson Place comes General Gaines Place, General Ledbetter Place, General Page Place, and General Wilkinson Place. Probably they were all generals in the Civil War days. We can even see Fort Gaines later today if we have time. It isn't far from the Estuarium."

"You are so right, Grampy," Clayton declared after typing in the generals' last names. "General Edmund Gaines, General Danville Ledbetter, General Richard Page, and General James Wilkinson. And, yes, Fort Gaines here on the island is named after General Edmund Gaines as is the City of Gainesville, in Florida.

"So much history around the Mobile area!" Mom reiterated. "Let's head back to the trolley stop."

After a short walk back to Cadillac Square, the group excitedly waited for the next trolley. "We will get off at Billy Goat Concessions and grab some lunch, before we see the Estuarium."

"YES, ready for that." Clayton and Austin both rubbed their stomachs.

"Hey, here comes Miss Martha and her trolley," Austin said.

"Hi there Grampy's group and Daisy," Miss Martha greeted. "How's your day going?"

"Oh, Miss Martha, you were right on about those Goat Trees... very weird," Clayton shivered.

At the very mention of goat trees, Daisy began shaking and wanted to get into Clayton's lap. "Hey, girl, it's okay, I promise," Clayton said while patting Daisy on the head.

"So where to now?" Miss Martha asked.

"We plan to get lunch at Billy Goat Concessions and then go to the Estuarium, If we have enough time, we'll also take in Fort Gaines," Austin said. "Do you have any more warnings for us?"

"Hmm...well...if you really want to know," Miss Martha opened her eyes wide and smiled sheepishly.

"The Estuarium is part of the Dauphin Island Sea Lab. You'll love that," Miss Martha told them. "Be careful about the stingray exhibit though. Visitors can touch the stingrays but are told to only use two fingers."

"Awesome!" Clayton exclaimed. "We saw lots of creatures at the aquarium in Newport, Kentucky, but these marine creatures here might be different from the ones at Newport."

"Well...just be careful," Miss Martha warned. "Some little girl last week didn't follow the rules and tried to catch a stingray, so, of course, all the stingrays started darting around like crazy. I guess they felt threatened. The workers had to shut down the exhibit. And naturally, the little girl got hysterical. So, PLEASE follow the rules about the stingrays and all the other interactive exhibits."

"Sure thing, Miss Martha," Clayton responded. "Any other warnings, like with GHOSTS? Daisy definitely felt some crazy vibes around the trees, and my buddy here, Austin, thought he saw the bride ghost!"

"Yes, ma'am, I saw something, looked like a lady in white clothes," Austin reiterated to Miss Martha and the group. "And, Grampy, here, well, he told us he saw a goat in a tree! Of course, none of us believed him since he is known for his jokes!"

Grampy held up his hands and just smiled.

"Okay, Grampy and group, I must warn you that Fort Gaines is considered the most haunted area on Dauphin Island. People report seeing Confederate and Union soldiers wandering around the grounds and guess what else? A lady in long flowing clothes!"

"Oh, dear!" replied Mom. "We promise to look out for that bride ghost."

"Here is your stop, you are almost to the end of Bienville Boulevard here at the far east end of the island," said Miss Martha. "You can easily walk to the concessions, the Sea Lab and Estuarium, and Fort Gaines."

"Thanks for your information," Grampy said as the group exited the trolley.

"You might also enjoy the walking trail at the Dauphin Island Bird Sanctuary, but keep away from those alligators!" Miss Martha hollered as she pulled away from the curb.

"Wow, alligators?" Austin questioned. "Did she just say alligators?"

As the group enjoyed hot dogs and chips at Billy Goat Concessions, Grampy read from his brochure about the Sea Lab's Estuarium, the Bird Sanctuary, and Fort Gaines.

"The Sea Lab's Estuarium has displays showing the four main habitats along the coast of Alabama. It contains 31 aquariums with over 100 different species.

There are Boardwalk Talks hosted by the marine researchers on the first and third Mondays."

"Yeh, today is the first Monday!" said Mom excitedly.

"Okay, a few words about the Bird Sanctuary," offered Grampy. "It covers 137 acres, has a three mile walking trail through forest land, marshes, and dunes. You can see migrating birds, fish, flowers, butterflies, and even alligators."

"Not so sure about those alligators, but the other things sound wonderful," Mom declared. "Grampy, what about Fort Gaines?"

"Fort Gaines is an historic fort best known for its role in the Battle of Mobile Bay during the American Civil War. It has original cannons used in the battle, pre-Civil War buildings, a blacksmith shop and kitchens, and tunnels to the corner bastions, plus a museum," Grampy said. "Sounds exciting to me, let's finish up our lunches and head on out. Let's switch off and go two and two because I doubt Daisy will be allowed in the Estuarium building. Two of us will take Daisy through the Bird Sanctuary while the other two will see the Estuarium, then we'll meet back here in 45 minutes and switch."

"Hey, Grampy, let's go see those birds and ALLIGATORS!" Clayton exclaimed as he checked Daisy's leash.

"Okay, guys, Austin and I will go and pet the stingrays and we promise to follow the rules!" Mom said as she stretched out two fingers ready to stroke them. "Everyone, synchronize your watches. It's 12:30, so we will meet here at 1:15 and switch destinations."

"Sounds like a plan, and then on to Ft. Gaines," Clayton said pretending he was loading a cannon.

—— **Chapter 7** ——
Grampy, We Won't Get Lost!

"Estuarium! Awesome!" Clayton beamed as he and Austin, Grampy and Mom met after their journeys.

Clayton showed how carefully he and Grampy had touched the stingrays.

"Yes, they felt so smooth," Austin said, "I could have spent the whole time at the stingray pool, but we wanted to see more fish and marine life exhibits. We were able to hear the researchers describe some of the projects they are investigating here on the island and in the coastal waters."

"My favorite thing was the trail at the Bird Sanctuary," marveled Mom. "So beautiful, and we stopped at the bridge over the lake and saw an ALLIGATOR! I wonder if the alligators ever get out of the water and wander along on the trail. Sure hope not."

"We didn't get to see an alligator there, but there were several cats who jumped out into the walkway and tried to scare Daisy," Clayton recalled. "We were so proud of her though! She actually started playing with the cats."

"No cats on our trail," Austin said. "Really glad we got to see the alligator in its natural environment though."

"Grampy, what was your favorite thing you and Mom saw?" Clayton asked.

"Everything was so nice, but I think my favorite thing was seeing all those marine creatures in the aquariums." Grampy pretended his hands were fish swimming around.

"Grampy, do we have time to visit Fort Gaines now?" Austin inquired.

"It is now 2:15, so we could probably check out Fort Gaines for about an hour," Grampy said as he checked his watch. "We need to be back to the *Granny Rose* by 4 o'clock, and then depart for the marina at Orange Beach. My friend, Scott, is picking us up there at 6 o'clock to go to dinner."

"Yeah! Let's move it on down the street!" Clayton pointed the way to Fort Gaines.

The group walked quickly to the entrance to Fort Gaines and they enthusiastically read the signs on the trail about the history of the fort.

"Look at this," Mom said. "The fort was established in 1821 and stood guard at the entrance to Mobile Bay during the Civil War and even in World War II. It was recently designated as one of the eleven Most Endangered Historic Sites in America due to the ongoing erosion from the Gulf of Mexico."

"Yes, I know, so much history in the Mobile area!" Grampy added. "Okay, group, let's split up again and meet back here at 3:30. Check your watches!"

"Okay, Grampy," said Austin. "Clayton, let's go check out the cannons and those tunnels to the bastions. Look over there, an anchor, HUGE!"

As Clayton and Austin headed for the Civil War gear, Mom and Grampy toured the blacksmith's shop, kitchen, museum, and gift shop, taking Daisy with them.

The time seemed to fly by while Clayton and Austin pretended they were soldiers.

"Soldier, full speed ahead, shoot those torpedoes!" Clayton hollered.

"Yes, sir, Captain Clayton," Austin answered. "Enemy hit!"

At 3:30, everyone met back at the entrance and relayed stories about the favorite things they saw at the fort.

"Those tunnels!" Austin and Clayton said together.

"No ghosts!" said Mom. "Seriously, my favorite thing was the museum, and you Grampy?"

"Hey, everyone knows I love history, so, it was the museum for me too. Let's stop and get an ice cream at Billy Goat Concessions and wait for the trolley to take us back to the pier."

"Sounds good, Grampy, and where is Mr. Scott taking us for dinner tonight?" asked Clayton.

"Some place called Lambert's Throwed Rolls," he answered. "Never been there but it sure has an interesting name."

After snacks and cold water to refill their water bottles, the group waited for the trolley.

"It's Miss Martha's trolley coming!" shouted Austin.

"How was everything?" Miss Martha inquired.

"Best thing was that none of us saw any ghosts," Mom marveled. "Really though, I enjoyed everything! We need to come back here to spend more time at the Estuarium, and I found out there is a four-hour excursion boat that travels out in the Gulf from Dauphin Island where you can fish as well as examine different marine life up close."

"Yes, the researchers on the boat are so knowledgeable about the coastal habitats," Miss Martha said. "Okay, here we go, back to the pier, right?"

"Right on," answered Clayton. "We have to journey over to Pirates Cove Marina at Orange Beach, and our friend, Mr. Scott, is taking us to a restaurant for dinner. Something about throwed rolls."

"Oh, my, that's Lambert's. Warning – watch out," Miss Martha laughed.

"Oh, no, please, no more ghosts," said Austin.

"Nothing like that. I am not telling you anything else. I definitely don't want to spoil the surprise." Miss Martha continued to smile and giggle.

Everyone bid Miss Martha good-bye and thanked her for her 'warnings.' The group followed Grampy down the dock to the *Granny Rose* where everyone helped prepare her for the hour trip over to Orange Beach.

"Hey, deckhands, I plan to use the GPS transponder as we cross Mobile Bay to Orange Beach. Have you studied longitude and latitude in your Social Studies class?"

"Yes," replied Clayton. "I remember the world is mapped off in angular degrees, minutes and seconds. Latitude is 0 degrees at the Equator and imaginary lines give the degrees north or south of the Equator from there. Longitude is the measure in degrees east or west of the Prime Meridian at Greenwich, England. These two readings are like your global address."

"It was a pretty awesome study at school," Austin added. "We were all even able to find the very location of our houses using the two coordinates of latitude and longitude on the transponder. Imagine that, even people on the other side of the world could find my house."

"Grampy, just wondering why we are going to use the GPS now, when we never used it on our river adventures?" Clayton asked.

"Mainly because on the rivers and Mobile Bay that we traveled today, we can still see the shores, and we wouldn't lose our way. Out in large bodies of water, it is helpful to use the GPS coordinates of your destination to make sure you stay on course to get there without getting lost."

"Here is our transponder, guys," Mom said, retrieving it from the storage cabinet at the wheelhouse.

"Cool!" Austin replied. "Will you teach us how to use it?"

"You bet," Mom said. "First of all, we have to know the coordinates for the Pirates Cove Marina, which is our next destination."

"I bought a special map of the Intracoastal Waterway that contains coordinates of the marinas along the way plus another important piece of information – where the fishing havens are located. That is how professional fishermen as well as everyday hobby fishermen are able to know where the best places to fish are located."

"Great! No wasting time dropping the hooks and just hoping for the best," Clayton said.

"Okay, guys, here are the Pirates Cove Marina coordinates," Grampy said. "30 degrees 19.215 latitude and 87 degrees 31.962 longitude."

"Let me show you how to enter this information into the transponder," Mom said, helping the boys.

"Got it, Grampy, we won't get lost!" Clayton said as he and Austin gave a thumbs up.

"All right! Here we go," Grampy answered, as he backed the *Granny Rose* out from the pier and steered toward the direction of Orange Beach.

"No torpedoes but full speed ahead!" Austin shouted.

Everyone was enjoying the relaxing trip to Orange Beach, even Daisy, who had curled up beside Clayton at his look-out post and promptly fell asleep.

However...Daisy woke up suddenly and barked toward the starboard side of the houseboat.

"There it is again, that antenna!" shouted Clayton. "LOOK!"

"Hey, sorry, Clayton, don't know what it was you saw," answered Grampy, shaking his head and rolling his eyes, as in disbelief.

"Whatever it was, Daisy knows it was there!" Clayton declared. He placed his hand on Daisy's head and petted her for the remainder of the trip, keeping a sharp eye on the starboard and port sides of the *Granny Rose*.

After pulling into Dock Number 11 at Pirates Cove Marina, the group readied themselves to check off houseboat arrival procedures on Grampy's list.

"Hey, Daisy, girl, I know you are tired. Sorry that thing...whatever it is, keeps bothering you," Clayton told her.

Daisy stretched, yawned, and followed Clayton to the wee-wee mat.

"Okay, deckhands, everything is A-OK," Grampy confirmed. "I will check us in for the night at the office and I'll call Scott and let him know we are back in case he wants to pick us up earlier than 6 o'clock."

Austin filled up Daisy's food bowl while Clayton cleaned her water bowl and added fresh water. Mom checked the supplies in the kitchen and walked to the marina grocery for a few more items.

"Scott will be here in 30 minutes," Grampy declared when he returned. "Let's shower and change into some fresh clothes for this adventure to the restaurant. I want to look good in case someone throws a roll and everyone there laughs at me."

Sure enough, just as Miss Martha had warned, the group walked into Lambert's and saw a server tossing rolls to customers.

"This place looks like fun!" Clayton shouted.

—— **Chapter 8** ——
Have Your Foghorn Ready!

"Good morning crew," Grampy greeted Clayton, Austin and Daisy as they climbed the ladder from their below-deck bunks to the main deck. "How about that delicious food last night? I was dreaming last night about rolls being tossed around and Clayton, you kept saying, 'something just hit me!' and Austin, you kept saying, 'more mashed potatoes, please!' every time the server came around with another bowl full."

"Wow, I didn't think I would want anything for breakfast after all that good food last night, but...well...there's always room for cereal and milk." Clayton laughed as he filled Daisy's food and water bowls and reached in the galley cabinet for his favorite cereal.

"Me, too," Austin agreed. "All that fried chicken and those mashed potatoes. I love my grandma's homemade rolls but I think those Lambert's rolls were better than hers. Of course, I wouldn't tell her that!"

"Definitely fun last night," Mom echoed the words of the others. "Let's all finish up breakfast. Big day ahead, following the Intracoastal Waterway to Perdido Key, Florida, where we are meeting Mr. Scott. He is taking us to the Naval Air Museum in Pensacola. How about after we get underway this morning, could you fellows search on the iPad about the waterway and the museum?"

"While you are searching, will you see if you can find out if the museum has an F-4 Phantom II plane on display there?" Grampy asked. "My very first job out of the United Electronics Institute in Louisville was building that kind of plane at the McDonnell Aircraft assembly plant in St. Louis, Missouri."

"A-OK," Clayton answered. "Grampy, will we need to enter the coordinates for the next marina on the transponder?"

"Yes, some parts of the waterway are very narrow and other parts are much more open. Here is the Intracoastal Waterway map and we will dock at the Holiday Harbor Marina."

"Okay," replied Clayton, "I found those coordinates, 30 degrees 18.758 latitude and 87 degrees 26.566 longitude. Mom, do you have the transponder?"

"Yes, how about you entering the information?" said Mom, handing the device to Clayton.

"Sure thing," Clayton said as he carefully typed in the numbers.

"Austin, would you call ahead to the marina to get our boat slip number for docking?" Grampy asked.

"Yes, sir, Captain Grampy!"

The crew finished breakfast, prepared the *Granny Rose* for disembarking, and got underway on their one hour trip to Perdido Key.

"Call to the Holiday Harbor Marina successful," Austin reported. "We have permission to pull into pier 6."

As the boys and Daisy assumed their look-out posts on the top deck, Clayton began searching about the Intracoastal Waterway and entered notes in his journal. Then Austin investigated and jotted down information about the National Naval Aviation Museum.

"Look how close we are to the shores!" Clayton exclaimed as they began waving to people along the way.

"Good morning, houseboat crew!" an elderly lady and gentleman shouted from the shore. "Where are you headed today?"

"Perdido Key and the Pensacola Naval Air Station," Austin answered.

"Best museum I ever saw, have fun. Maybe you will get to see the Blue Angels practice," advised the lady.

On the other shore, there was a young couple with two dogs on leashes sitting at an outdoor restaurant. Daisy immediately took notice and barked what must have been a friendly greeting to the other dogs who then barked a 'hello' back at Daisy.

"Love your dog," they said to Clayton and Austin. "She sure is cute."

"Thanks, and yours too," answered Clayton.

"We just got a warning that fog might form this morning on the waterway. Be careful, have your foghorn ready just in case," called another customer at the restaurant.

"Yes, we have it ready," Austin said, "thanks."

A little further along on the journey, the waterway became wider and it was too far to talk to the shore dwellers. Grampy was careful to keep the *Granny Rose* centered between the buoys anchored in the water.

"Grampy, big log ahead on the starboard side!" yelled Clayton.

"Got it in sight," Grampy answered as he steered the houseboat and avoided the log.

"Uh-oh!" Austin shouted. "Fog rolling in!"

"Can't see a thing, this fog is so dense. It came in so quickly," Grampy said.

"Hey, deckhands, listen for any boat motor sound," Mom suggested. "If you hear that noise, start using the foghorn to warn the other boater you are in the area."

"Yes, ma'am, got it right here," Austin replied.

"Hear that?"shouted Clayton. "Another boat approaching! It's getting louder."

"Yes," answered Austin, who then blew the foghorn three times.

"Okay, the boat motor has slowed down. They must have heard you," said Clayton, with relief in his voice.

"Wow, that was a close call!" Grampy said.

Just as quickly as the fog had rolled in, it dispersed and there was a full view ahead for the remainder of the trip to Perdido Key and the Holiday Harbor Marina. Grampy and the crew prepared the houseboat for docking, checking off the list of arrival procedure duties.

"Great, we are ahead of schedule, even with the dense fog slowing us down," Mom commented. "Mr. Scott will be here in about 30 minutes."

"I'll check us in at the marina office," Grampy said.

"Hey, fellas, did you have a chance to check out the Intracoastal Waterway and the Naval Air Museum on the iPad while we were traveling?" asked Mom.

"Oh, yeah!" Clayton beamed. "When can we tell you all about our newly-found knowledge?"

—— Chapter 9 ——
I Can See the Pilot!

"Hi, Mr. Scott," Clayton smiled. "We are ready for more adventures today. Mom said Austin and I can share our research findings about the Intracoastal Waterway and the Naval Air Museum with everyone – well – we have to wait until we are in your car and on our way."

"Great, proud of you two young men," Mr. Scott answered. "I'll be interested to hear your investigation results."

"I'll get Daisy settled in her kennel," Clayton said as he patted Daisy. "We'll be back in a few hours."

The group disembarked from the *Granny Rose* and made their way down the pier to Mr. Scott's car for the short trip to Pensacola.

"Okay, you young investigators, tell us about your research," Grampy said.

"The Intracoastal Waterway," Clayton cleared his throat and spoke up so everyone in the car could hear him. He opened his journal and reviewed his notes.

"It is a 3000 mile inland waterway along the coastlines of the Atlantic Ocean and Gulf of Mexico, running from Boston, Massachusetts southward and around the southern tip of Florida. Then it follows the Gulf Coast to Brownsville, Texas. It is helpful to boaters because it provides a more easily traveled route - more tranquil waters than the open sea. Its nicknames are the 'Big C' and the 'Great Loop.' In order to have more trade and commerce to help grow and bind the new nation of the United States, in the early 1800's, U.S. Treasury Secretary Albert Gallatin presented a plan for its future transportation needs. In 1826, the U.S. Congress authorized the first survey for an inland canal, thus paving the way for the Intracoastal Waterway.

Today the waterway is overseen by the U.S. Army Corps of Engineers. Federal law provides for the depth to be maintained at 12 feet, but limited funding has prevented that in all sections of the waterway. Some areas are only 7 to 9 feet deep. The waterway provides commercial transport of goods as well as recreation for pleasure boaters. Boaters in the ocean also use the waterway when the seas are too rough for safe travel."

"Good to know all that," Mr. Scott said, nodding his approval to Clayton. "I have a niece, Julie, and her husband, Walt, who purchased a sailboat and traveled the waterway and the open seas from New Orleans to Wilmington, North Carolina, where they keep it docked now. The trip took them 14 days."

"Did they only use the waterway when the ocean was rough?" Austin asked.

"Yes, for the most part, they were in the ocean and let the wind carry them along, although the boat has two motors for when there is no wind. Their top speed was 6 to 8 knots. They used the GPS coordinates to stay their course."

"Not a pleasant question, but I just have to ask…did they ever get seasick? Also, how long did the journey take?" Mom asked.

"Julie told me they never got sick in the waterway, but did get sick while in the ocean. She said there was only one time when they became really scared. It was at sea, and the winds became really excessive, and they could see lots of lightning. She and Walt decided to get their 'ditch bag' ready just in case they were tossed out of the boat or if they needed to 'ditch' the boat and climb into their dingy."

"A ditch bag!" Clayton exclaimed. "So, what was in it?"

"I haven't actually seen it, but she said it was a very small bag and contained a little food and important identification papers. By the way, they never had to use it and the storm went on its way."

"Whew…" Austin said, wiping his forehead.

"Okay, Austin, we are almost to the Naval Air Station," Mr. Scott said, "tell us about your research."

"Alright, here goes…The National Naval Aviation Museum, located in Pensacola, Florida, is the world's largest Naval Aviation museum. It has more than 150 restored aircraft from the Navy, Marine Corps, and the Coast Guard. The exhibits also contain uniforms and historic documents. They have a giant screen theater and flight simulators, plus a flight deck where you can get the sensation of standing on the deck of an aircraft carrier, AND guess what? You can actually climb up and sit in a model of a Blue Angel aircraft! AND THAT'S NOT ALL! They have a 4-D Theater where you actually feel like you are a part of the Blue Angels performance. The Blue Angel demonstration team was formed in 1946. Today they fly six F/A-18 Hornet planes. The highest speed they fly during a show is 700 miles per hour and the lowest is 120 miles per hour. WOW! And, yes, Grampy, there is an exhibit with the F-4 Phantom II aircraft."

"I'm ready...up, up, and away," Clayton said as he pretended to fly.

"You found out some really interesting facts," Grampy said. Good job on your research, Austin, and I am glad to know they have a plane like I made!"

"I checked the Blue Angels Practice and Show times, and nothing was listed for today," said Mr. Scott, "but you never know, I've seen them up in the air even when they weren't actually on the schedule. We will be able to see what a Blue Angel plane looks like though – up close and personal."

"Let's do this thing!" Austin said excitedly as Mr. Scott entered the museum grounds.

After exiting the car and snapping some photos outside the museum, the group successfully passed through the security checkpoint. They were immediately thrust into excitement as they saw the replicas of Blue Angels aircraft. Clayton and Austin quickly but carefully climbed the ladders to sit in the planes.

"Is the target locked in?" Clayton asked.

"Yes, Captain Clayton," replied Austin.

After more 'piloting,' the boys descended the ladder and examined the brochure and map from the museum.

"This place is huge and we may need to split up if we all want to have time to peruse those exhibits we would like to see," Grampy said.

"Good idea," said Mr. Scott. "Let's meet at the café entrance at 11:30."

"Got it," Clayton replied as he and Austin synchronized the time on their watches with Grampy's watch.

The boys headed off to the area of the flight simulators and the 4-D theater while Mom, Grampy, and Mr. Scott wound their way to the F-4 Phantom II exhibit.

"Wow, now I am really confused after seeing all these exhibits," Austin said when the group came back together at the café.

"What's got you stumped?" Mom asked.

"Last summer we toured the General Patton Museum at Fort Knox in Kentucky and it was so cool to sit in those tanks. Then, we toured the battleship at the Battleship Memorial Park in Mobile, plus got to go aboard that submarine. Now, we get to sit in fighter planes. Just not sure what I might like the best...Army...Navy...tanks...   subs...airplanes...and then...well maybe...I would like to do something else when I get older." Austin shook his head and rubbed his hands.

"Luckily, you don't have to make a decision today, young man," Mr. Scott said. Who knows? You have the 8th grade to finish and then four years of high school to think about a career path."

"Know how you feel, man, maybe I'll be a gourmet chef. I do love to eat," Clayton laughed.

"Yes, yes, yes, but most of the time you order burgers!" Mom replied.

"Speaking of burgers, let's order lunch," Clayton suggested.

After lunch and more touring, the group headed back to Mr. Scott's car.

"Hey, that was just fantastic!" Grampy said. "We didn't cover everything, will have to return here another time."

"Hey, gang, would you like to take in the beach for a little while over by my condo? Then we could view the sun going down at the Sunset Grille. It is located right by your marina. That is the very best place to view sunsets...at least in my opinion. And that is the whole wide world, not just Florida."

"Yes, sir," Clayton answered. "We brought our swim clothes and towels with us today."

"Sounds like a plan," Mr. Scott declared.

After a short car ride to Perdido Key, the boys were changing into their swim attire when Mr. Scott's 10th floor condo began shaking and the windows rattled. The noise outside got louder, louder, LOUDER!

"Get out on the deck, gang, boys hurry up," yelled Mr. Scott, "sounds like the Blue Angels coming!"

"Here we come!" answered Clayton as he and Austin finished dressing and ran to join the others on the deck.

"LOOK, I CAN SEE THE PILOT!" shouted Clayton.

"We were even with them," Austin said, looking totally amazed. "We were even with them," he said again, placing his hand and arm in a straight position outward. "They were right outside this window, right there!" Austin pointed out the window.

"They're gone," Mom concluded as the noise died down, the windows no longer rattled, and the floor felt secure.

"Yes, when they come over, you better look up fast because they are way past you in a second," Mr. Scott declared.

"Do windows ever break from the noise?" Clayton asked.

"No," answered Mr. Scott. "The planes are not allowed to fly at speeds that would break windows. They do not break the sound barrier here."

"AWESOME!" announced Clayton.

—— Chapter 10——
Sneaky Pete & the Yellow Submarine

After an afternoon of swimming and paddleboarding at Perdido Key Beach, Clayton and Austin were unable to stop talking about the sights and sounds of the Blue Angels.

"Have you ever felt anything like that condo shaking?" Austin asked. "I have never been anywhere near an earthquake. I wonder if it feels like that?"

"Yeah, man, I wonder too," answered Clayton.

The boys exited the water, collected their belongings on the beach, and began to walk back to Mr. Scott's condo.

"Hey, Austin, WAIT UP! Look out there in the water!" shouted Clayton. "It's that antenna-looking thing, well...whatever it is...sticking out of the water again. See it?"

"I caught a glimpse of it, buddy!" Austin marveled.

"Alright...so now you know I am not just seeing illusions. What could it be?" Clayton asked.

"Wait a minute... didn't your Grampy say his friend, Mr. Sneaky Pete, lived in Destin? Remember, the one who owns a yellow submarine?" Austin asked.

"YES!" Clayton bellowed. "That's got to be it. Grampy probably told Mr. Pete about us."

"You know how Grampy loves to play jokes," Austin replied. "Do you think he asked his friend to follow us along as we traveled?"

"I guess Sneaky Pete is a good name for him," Clayton laughed. "We really must hint around to Grampy about us meeting him."

"A yellow submarine? He owns a yellow submarine, man! That's too cool!" Austin kept shaking his head in disbelief. "Maybe we could do some research about submarines on the iPad and just casually relay a hint to Grampy about how awesome it would be to actually ride in one, not just see one."

"Great idea, dude," Clayton responded as they entered the elevator to ride up to Mr. Scott's condo. "I'll be glad to get back to the *Granny Rose* so we can check on Daisy."

"I second that!" Austin agreed.

"Next year, man!" Clayton exclaimed, as he and Austin opened the door to the condo where Mom, Grampy, and Mr. Scott were relaxing on the deck. "Gotta come back here to visit again, see more sights at Mobile, Dauphin Island, and the Naval Air Museum. Right, Mom, right Grampy?"

"Absolutely," Austin agreed. "And we still have more adventures to come. It will be great to see your dad, and my mom and dad when we get to Destin tomorrow evening. Do you think we can successfully lobby them to come back for two weeks next summer?"

"You got me onboard with that," Grampy acknowledged .

"Me, too, guys," Mom agreed.

"Everybody ready to head back to the houseboat?" Mr. Scott asked.

"A-OK," the youngsters answered.

"Okay, you guys can get cleaned up back at the *Granny Rose*. We'll check on Daisy, eat some fish sandwiches at the Sunset Grille and take in the beauty of the Florida sunset," Mr. Scott said.

"Sounds like a plan!" Austin said, "And Clayton and I have some research to do on the iPad, don't we, good buddy?"

"Wow, so impressed!" Grampy smiled. "What about?"

"Submarines," Clayton answered with a big grin.

As the group was on their way back to Holiday Harbor Marina and the *Granny Rose*, Grampy and Mom continued to marvel at the beauty of the area while Clayton and Austin read about subs on the iPad and took notes in their journals.

"Oh yes," Mr. Scott added. "Do you guys want to hear a little bit of history about Pensacola and the Perdido Key area?"

"Sure," Clayton said, "It wouldn't surprise me to learn that this area has a similar history as Mobile and Dauphin Island."

"So right," Mr. Scott responded. "The first known native tribes were the Muskogean and Creek. Spanish explorer, Tristan de Luna, founded a settlement in 1559. It changed leadership several times as Europeans competed for the land. England ruled in the late 1700's and established strong fortifications, but the Spanish again captured the Pensacola area. In the early 1800's, Spain and the United States negotiated a treaty whereby the U.S. bought the Floridas for $5 million. The Confederacy was in charge during the

Civil War with Fort Barrancas and Fort Pickens providing strategic places for the Confederates to try to occupy. Of course, the Union soldiers eventually took over the forts, and the area was under the control of the United States again after the Civil War ended."

"When we get back here, like... maybe...next summer," Clayton displayed that 'OH, PLEASE SAY YES' look on his face to Mom and Grampy. "We could visit more historic forts."

"Grampy, we know you love the study of history," Austin added.

"YES, YES, YES, I hear your hints loud and clear," Grampy responded.

"By the way, Grampy, since Austin and I have been researching about submarines, Mr. Sneaky Pete might like to talk to us about his experiences with subs. You know, he might like to try to influence us to join the Navy in a few years and work on the subs."

"Yes sir, Grampy, we want to learn all we can about subs. Like what the modern ones LOOK like and how they work, and even what it feels like to actually RIDE in one," Austin said with those big, sparkling eyes and the face that also said 'OH, PLEASE SAY YES.'

"Wow, Grampy, how awesome it would be to sing about a yellow submarine when we are onboard a real yellow submarine." Clayton began humming the tune of the song. "Then we could actually see that periscope going up and down in the water."

"Grampy, guess what, I actually saw an antenna sticking out of the water a while ago, so...Clayton hasn't been just seeing illusions," Austin said. "Up periscope! Down periscope!" Austin moved his arms up and down as if holding a periscope and pretended to look through a screen at an approaching enemy sub.

"You don't think Sneaky Pete is responsible for that thing that comes up out of the water that looks like an antenna, do you?" Grampy smiled, laughed, and shrugged his shoulders.

"You just gave away the joke, Grampy," Clayton said, shaking his finger at him. "We know your look, that smile, that laugh that means you're up to something."

—— **Chapter 11** ——
Docking Next to the Yellow Submarine

"Thank you, Mr. Scott, for showing us around the Panhandle area," Clayton said, as Mr. Scott was leaving to go back to his condo.

"Yes, I second that," said Austin.

"And Scott, thanks for bringing us here to the Sunset Grille to take pictures of the sunset," Mom added. "Gorgeous!"

"Yes, great to see you, Scott, and thanks for taking us around in your car. I'll be catching up with you later in the winter from my warm weather home, the *Granny Rose*. We'll be leaving here in the morning to travel on the Intracoastal Waterway to Destin," Grampy said.

"You will pass through Navarre Beach on your journey," Mr. Scott said. "Too bad you don't have time to stop and fish there because Navarre has the longest pier in the Gulf. Also, you need to plan to dock somewhere in Destin for tomorrow night because there is no public docking from Navarre Beach to the

Fort Walton and Destin areas. The area is all under the control of Eglin Air Force Base. It covers more than 400,000 acres and is the home of the 96th Test Wing of the Air Force. It is the test and evaluation center for air navigation, guidance, and weapons systems and is a major training facility. You might even see some troopers rappelling out of helicopters as you travel through the area. It is one of only a few U. S. Government bases where there is a public airport on the government owned land. It's the Destin and Fort Walton Airport."

"That is where my parents flew into on Monday," Austin commented. "And your Dad, too, Clayton buddy."

"Hey, can't wait to see them all tomorrow night," grinned Clayton. "Grampy, do you have confirmation of Sydney and Camryn and their families' arrival in Destin?"

"I will call them in the morning and confirm, but we texted about all of us going on the *Buccaneer* Pirate Cruise tomorrow night for dinner complete with all the fun antics of the pirates," Grampy answered.

"Okay, great, big day tomorrow," Mom said excitedly.

After all the good-byes with Mr. Scott, Grampy and his group checked the supplies for the next day, made their phone calls to family members and were making their way to their bunks. Daisy seemed incredibly excited and not quite her normal self.

"Grampy," Clayton called as the boys climbed down to their below deck bunk. "Sure would be nice to see that yellow submarine tomorrow!"

"Oh yes, I agree, it would be nice to see a yellow submarine," Grampy hollered back and his hearty laughter could be heard by the boys.

Daisy began to bark, climbed into Clayton's bunk, and dug under the covers.

"What's up, girl?" Clayton inquired. "When we talked about the yellow submarine, did you get scared?" Clayton patted Daisy's head as she poked her nose and eyes out from the blanket. "It's okay, no ghosts, just a submarine with a periscope sticking out above the water. Good night, girl." Clayton tried to soothe Daisy, but her panting continued, along with her restlessness.

Neither Clayton nor Austin slept well that night. Daisy finally calmed down as she fell asleep nestled on top of Clayton's stomach.

"It's that time!" The boys heard Grampy's bellowing from the above deck. "The sun is coming up! Time to get the *Granny Rose* underway!"

"Pancakes ready!" Mom called.

"Magic words for me." Austin opened his eyes wide and quickly got dressed for the day.

"Oh, wow, can it be morning already?" Clayton yawned, as he changed into his jeans and shirt and put on his shoes. "Come on Daisy, let's go to the wee-wee mat and get your food ready."

"Guess what?" Grampy asked as the boys and Daisy finished climbing the ladder to the middle deck. "I have great news!"

"Mr. Sneaky Pete will be in Destin?" Clayton inquired with a hopeful look on his face.

"Maybe, maybe not!" Grampy laughed. "But I do know that Camryn and her family and Sydney and her family arrived in Destin yesterday and will be joining up with us later today for the *Buccaneer* Pirate Cruise. Clayton, your dad is making the reservations for everyone on the cruise tonight. And Jim and Samantha obtained permission for us to dock the *Granny Rose* at the Destin Plantation Marina in the Destin Harbor.

"Alright! Yes, that is great news!" Clayton pumped his fists. "Daisy, did you hear that? We get to see our fellow deckhands, Camryn and Sydney!"

Daisy caught the excitement as she ran around in circles and when Clayton and Austin bent down to pat her, she turned over on her back so they could stroke her belly.

"Breakfast eaten, guys?" Mom asked as she began clearing away the dirty dishes.

"Yes, well...almost, give me a minute please, Mom, you know I am a growing boy and need all the nourishment I can get!" Clayton eagerly ate the last bite of his pancakes.

"I'm ready!" Austin exclaimed. "Let's get this show on the road! Well...get the show on the Intracoastal Waterway! I can't wait to see Mom and Dad tonight.

Grampy, I will start checking our departure procedures for our 'mansion on the water' and secure the galley cabinets."

"Thanks, Deckhand Austin. After we get underway, maybe you and Deckhand Clayton could assume your lookout posts and research on your iPad about the history of Destin."

"Sure will, plus we want to finish our research about submarines."

"And research about finding underwater treasure!" Clayton added.

"Do you intend to search for treasure on this trip?" Mom asked.

"Well, Mom and Grampy, we want to be prepared...well...just in case...you never know when Mr. Sneaky Pete will surface in his yellow submarine. He might even have found some shipwreck while he was sneaking around in the waters following us the last several days," Clayton said with that hopeful look on his face.

"Now, don't get those hopes up too high!" Grampy cautioned, with that sparkle in his eyes.

"Something's up," whispered Austin to Clayton.

"You're right on that," Clayton responded.

After the crew checked off all the jobs on the departure list and Grampy backed out from the marina space, Clayton, Austin, and Daisy assumed their posts on the top deck while Mom and Grampy kept watch from the wheelhouse.

"Okay, Austin buddy, let's finish researching from that site we found about shipwrecks and locating marine artifacts and treasure and then investigate about the history of Destin," Clayton said as they retrieved their iPad and journals.

The day was lazily spent rambling down the waterway. The group passed several other boats on the waterway, waving and having conversations with the occupants. "Where are you headed?" was the favorite greeting. Daisy barked in a friendly way and wagged her tail as she spied other dogs on the watercraft. After Clayton and Austin finished their research, they continued to dream of finding treasure and even jotted down some ideas for an underwater adventure story.

"Getting close," Grampy called up to the youngsters. "The William T. Marler Bridge is in sight."

"Got it, Grampy, we are coming down," Austin responded.

"We'll start checking off the docking procedures," Clayton said.

As Clayton, Austin, and Mom examined and carefully prepared the buoys and ropes, Grampy slowed the engine.

"Don't want to create a large wake as we enter the Destin Harbor," Grampy commented. The marina at Jim and Samantha's will be coming into view shortly."

"Clayton, look dude, do you see what I see?" Austin placed the binoculars up to his eyes. "THERE IS A YELLOW SOMETHING IN THE WATER UP THERE!"

"OH MAN, OH MAN! I SEE IT!" Clayton yelled as he took a turn using the binoculars.

Slowly, slowly, Grampy guided the *Granny Rose* further into the Destin Harbor.

"There's Jim and Samantha!" Mom pointed out. "Do you see them waving to us, Deckhand Clayton and Deckhand Austin?"

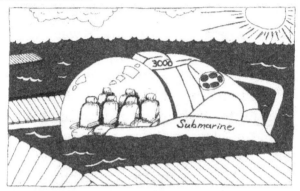

"Yes, and what is that yellow thing in the water?" Clayton asked.

"Could it be what we think it is?" Austin yelled.

"And there is a man standing there with Mr. Jim and Mrs. Samantha. That must be Mr. Pete, and that must be his yellow submarine," Clayton said as his eyes got larger.

"Prepare to dock," yelled Grampy, as he piloted their houseboat into the marina slip right next to the yellow watercraft.

"Grampy, are we docking here? FOR REAL?" Clayton questioned.

Chapter 12
Is That a Shipwreck?

"Mom, look, there comes Dad! And Austin, there's your mom and dad!" Clayton pointed to the pier.

"Can't wait to tell them about our adventures on this trip," Austin said.

"Grampy, that man standing by that yellow vessel is waving to you. Is he the mysterious Mr. Pete with his yellow submarine? It must be. I see *Sneaky Pete* written on the side of his vessel," Clayton observed.

"Sure thing," laughed Grampy, as he, Clayton, Austin, and Mom successfully completed the docking of the *Granny Rose*.

As everyone greeted and hugged each other, Pete, Clayton and Austin patted Daisy as she barked and jumped by the yellow sub.

"Daisy, it's fine, girl! We are safe and that yellow vessel won't hurt you," Mr. Pete calmly told Daisy as he rubbed her head. Still panting but sitting on the pier at Clayton's feet, Daisy seemed to be relaxing.

"There it is, Clayton, look, man! That thing you kept seeing poking up out of the water." Austin pointed to the antenna on top of the sub.

"Yes, I just have to ask you, Mr. Pete, did Grampy give you the idea to follow us in the water for the last several days?" Clayton inquired.

Mr. Pete and Grampy both shrugged their shoulders but with those guilty grins on their faces, Clayton knew he was right.

"Grampy, what are we going to do about you and your jokes?" Austin just shook his head.

"Well, guess you youngsters will have to give Grampy another trial like you did on your last cruise when you discovered he was the trickster," Mr. Jim suggested.

"Okay," the boys agreed.

"I have an idea, fellows," said Mr. Pete. "Let's sentence Grampy to go along on an underwater adventure with us in the *Sneaky Pete*. He was an Army man, not a Navy man, probably never been underwater."

"YES!" the boys shouted.

"Well, let's get everyone settled for lunch in our condo," Mrs. Samantha said. "Then Mr. Pete can show us his yellow submarine."

Everyone was singing the yellow submarine song as they followed Mrs. Samantha into the condo.

"So happy to be in Destin," Mom said. "It is so beautiful here."

"And thanks for piloting the houseboat from Paducah to Mobile for us," Grampy said.

"Yes, it was great learning about the history of the Mobile and Pensacola areas and our visits to Dauphin Island and the Naval Air Museum were spectacular," Clayton added.

"We have jotted down so many notes on this trip in our journals, we should write a story," Austin chimed in. "Call it 'The Adventures of Clayton and Austin.' How about it, Clayton buddy?"

"I'm in," Clayton agreed. "Who knows, we might even write about an underwater adventure where we find treasure."

As everyone was enjoying their soup and sandwiches, they kept asking Mr. Pete about his tour of duty on a U. S. Navy submarine and why in the world he would want to purchase a sub.

"Yes, when the yellow submarine was put up for sale, my wife and I just had to go for it. We actually met years ago when I was stationed aboard a Navy sub and we have always enjoyed singing the 'yellow submarine' song. I really enjoyed my time in the Navy. I volunteered for sub duty because I got paid more money for that assignment. Fortunately, I never suffered from claustrophobia and I considered it 'my office with no windows.' All of the men assigned to the sub became a close-knit group because we all got to know each other well. You never knew when you might be eating breakfast sitting next to the Captain or exercising with the Chief Executive Officer. Sometimes on the large ships, especially aircraft carriers, you might not get to meet everyone because there are so many sailors onboard. Everyone on our vessel got to train on each other's jobs, so if someone got sick while we were out on assignment, another sailor could readily step in to cover the position. Everyone especially had to learn fire-fighting and emergency responses. Our time on the sub involved six hours on duty, six hours off work and six hours sleeping. Then the cycle started again. Three of us shared two bunks as one of us was working, one man was off duty, and one man was sleeping. Several years ago, subs were diesel powered, but today's Navy subs are nuclear powered."

"How incredibly organized," commented Mom. "What did you do on your time off duty?"

"We watched movies, played cards or board games, exercised with punching bags, resistance bands, treadmills and stationery bikes. We were not allowed to lift weights because if someone dropped a weight, it would make a noise that an enemy vessel might hear underwater. Thus, we would give away our position."

"Such an awesome life," Clayton said with a face that showed disbelief.

"What is the most special thing you remember about all the sights you experienced on your assignments?" asked Grampy.

"At night, when we were above water, and there were calm seas and stars were out, there would be an eerie-looking, glowing green trail coming from the sub over the water. It was caused by a reflection from the nighttime sky on the sub."

"Wow, that is special. Clayton, that sounds like another chapter for our book," Austin said. "Maybe titled, 'The Monster from the Green Trail' or something like that. We could have an underwater creature creep above water from the green trail. What do you think?"

"Sounds like a possibility, good buddy," Clayton said as he made creeping around movements with his arms and fingers along with making a scary looking face.

"Would you young investigators like to share about your research on the history of Destin?" asked Mom.

"We're on it, Mom," Clayton answered. "Austin, you want to go first?"

"Similar to the other areas where we have been on this trip, the Destin area was inhabited by Native American tribes as many artifacts from their culture have been found in the area. It is recorded that Spanish seamen led by Panfilo de Narvaez came ashore in 1528 and Spanish explorer, Don Francisco Milan Tapia, and his group investigated the area between what is now Mobile and Pensacola. He kept a journal that described the area and drew a small sketch in it showing an outlying island sand dune and lots of pine trees. This is apparently the first known picture of what became Destin. It was named for Captain Leonard Destin of New London, Connecticut, who began sailing and fishing in Gulf waters around 1835, and made a permanent settlement here about 1845. The settlers were known for their fishing, and the Destin History and Fishing Museum documents the development of the fishing industry.

"Okay, your turn, Clayton."

"I'm on it," replied Clayton. "The Destin-Gulf Coast Deep Sea Fishing Rodeo was begun in the late 1940's and has grown to attract as many as 30,000 anglers during the month long event in October. It is now called the Destin Fishing Rodeo, and participants from toddlers to teens to seniors compete in various categories. Today, Destin has the largest charter fishing fleet in Florida. Destin is known as the 'world's luckiest fishing village.' The story is told that Leroy Collins, Governor of Florida, was headed to the State Fair in Pensacola in 1956 and stopped in Destin during the time of the Fishing Rodeo. With a tight schedule to maintain that day, the governor accompanied a local angler named Captain Salty for a 15 minute ocean trip. Governor Collins caught a 20 pound king mackerel during that 15 minutes and then dubbed Destin as the 'world's luckiest fishing village.' That name became official in October, 1956. The Destin area has continued to grow in population, and the town is also noted for its white sandy beaches."

"Wow, you guys found some great articles in your research," applauded Mr. Jim.

"I have heard and read about some other families who settled in Destin in its early days of the 1900's," added Mrs. Samantha. "There were the Kellys, the Calhouns, and the Marlers among them. I have a friend, Sharon, who works at Shoreline Towers, and her great-grandfather was William T. Marler, of one of the founding families."

"And when you travel around here, Fort Walton, and down Hwy. 98 and 30A to Panama City Beach, you will find lots of streets named after the founding families," added Mr. Jim.

After a round of high-fives with the boys, Mr. Jim and Mrs. Samantha began clearing away the lunch dishes.

"So...when do we get to actually tour this sub of yours?" Grampy asked.

"I am ready whenever you are, group," Mr. Pete said excitedly. "But, first, I have a special gift for Daisy. Grampy told me about your incredible dog so I purchased something I hope she will like and hopefully, she won't be afraid of the yellow sub anymore."

"Daisy, did you hear that? A present for you," Clayton clapped.

Mr. Pete pulled a dog collar from his jacket pocket.

"Look, it's a dog collar with yellow submarines on it," Austin exclaimed.

Everyone had a huge laugh and clapped while Clayton changed Daisy's collar to the new yellow submarine one. Daisy jumped around and wagged her tail in approval.

"Well, come on, Daisy, let's go take a ride in the yellow submarine," Mr. Pete led her and the group downstairs and to the dock.

"Welcome to the *Sneaky Pete*," Mr. Pete said as he opened the hatch and pulled down the railing so the passengers could board easily. "There's room for six passengers, so...let's see, which six passengers should be first?"

"I vote for Daisy," Clayton declared.

"I second that," Austin agreed.

"Since Clayton, Austin, and Daisy come as a package deal, that makes three passengers, Pete makes four, and I'll be glad to wait for the second trip," Grampy volunteered with a skeptical sound in his voice.

"A little hesitant, are you?" Mom grinned at Grampy. "Okay, we'll give you some time to ponder that idea. I will wait for the second trip so I can give Grampy an extra push to board this thing. Austin, how about your mom and dad go with you boys and Daisy?"

"We are ready, willing, and able for this adventure," Austin's dad responded.

As the first group took their seats in the *Sneaky Pete*, Mr. Pete explained it had an acrylic cabin, was powered by lithium batteries, could be underwater for eight hours, had an oxygen delivery system with oxygen sensors and a backup breathing system, could dive up to 1000 meters, and had a maximum speed of three knots.

"We feel very safe, don't we Daisy?" Clayton said, while placing a seatbelt around Daisy. He sat in a seat close to her in the cabin as a 'just in case she gets scared' measure.

"Clayton and I did some research about subs and we found out that subs go back as far as the Revolutionary War days," Austin explained. "The first sub to use torpedoes was in the 1870's, and wars have been fought differently since then. Today's subs carry nuclear warheads. They can stay underwater as long as they have food with their modern oxygen delivery systems. They even have special equipment to remove salt from ocean water so they will have access to fresh water."

"And we even found out what to do if we locate any underwater treasure," Clayton advised. "Well, we weren't sure if we would get to ride in a sub, but when we realized it had to be you and your yellow sub that followed us along on our trip in Mobile Bay and the Intracoastal Waterway, well...we were hoping anyway, that we could ride, so we researched treasure searching, well...just in case."

"Glad you did!" Mr. Pete replied. "Things change underwater all the time because of the winds and currents making the water move around. It is possible to see all kinds of marine artifacts at the bottom in the sand. People come here to Florida all the time to search for underwater treasure. It could be very profitable, but most people go home empty-handed. As a matter of fact, after Hurricane Michael came through the Florida Panhandle this year, there were shipwrecks that washed up on shore at Dog Island. They were unearthed from an 1899 hurricane in that area. Since we had a storm here last night, who knows what we might see underwater today?"

"Yes, just what we wanted to hear, right Clayton?" Austin asked.

"Ready, set, explore!" Clayton answered as Mr. Pete got underway with the *Sneaky Pete* and they began descending.

"Look, there is a school of beautiful fish," exclaimed Austin's mom.

"And all those turtles," said Austin's dad.

"We aren't very far from the coast, but we will dive a little deeper in the water so you can see the bottom of the Gulf here," Mr. Pete advised.

"Oh, my, are we slowing down, Mr. Pete?" asked Austin.

"Yes, the deeper you go, the slower you travel. The water becomes denser as we dive, and it holds us back."

"Mr. Pete, Mr. Pete, I see something!" shouted Clayton. "It looks like part of an anchor off an old boat. Is it a SHIPWRECK?"

"Yes, I see that, could be part of the hull of an ancient vessel," Mr. Pete answered.

"Do you think there is any...TREASURE stuck in the sand?" Austin stammered.

"Not sure," but I will record the coordinates and we can report this to the Florida authorities," Mr. Pete said.

"Oh yes, too bad, we can't take anything," Clayton shook his head. "We learned you aren't supposed to take anything from an underwater find. The site is supposed to be reported to the Bureau of Archaeological Research with the Florida Department of State. Historic things like anchors and cannons are found often in the Florida waters. They will investigate to see if the discovery has been documented previously or is a new find."

"Wow, you guys were really ready for treasure hunting! Proud of you and your research," Austin's mom commented.

"I will use our special camera to photograph the site and will record the coordinates so we can report the find to the Bureau for their consideration. They will have your names, Clayton and Austin, and they will further communicate with you about the authenticity of a new find."

"YEAH!" Clayton beamed. "You mean we might be famous even though we are only in 8th grade?"

"MR. PETE! THERE IS SOMETHING SHINY LAYING IN THE SAND, DO YOU SEE IT?" Austin marveled. "Can we move over that way to get a closer view?

"THERE IS A STACK OF SHINY THINGS!" Clayton added. "OLD COINS FROM AN OLD SPANISH GALLEON?"

"Totally thrilling," replied Mr. Pete. "Could be an old, old treasure box from a shipwreck. I will guide the vessel as close as I can so we can get the best possible pictures. I read that the United Nations has estimated there have been over 3,000,000 shipwrecks around the world over the years. Maybe we found another one."

"Oh, wow, not only might you youngsters get famous, but rich too," commented Austin's dad.

"Yes, don't forget us little people when you get rich and famous," laughed Mr. Pete. "I'm heading back to the surface now so we can pick up our next group of passengers. After their ride, we will place a call to the Florida Department of State in Tallahassee."

"Mr. Pete, can't wait to tell our family and friends... and... is it okay with you if... well, it would so exciting...if...Austin and I place the call to the Florida authorities?" Clayton asked.

Chapter 13
Too Many Choices

"Well, I have to admit I am thrilled to be back at the dock," Grampy said as he exited the *Sneaky Pete.* "The sights and those archeological artifacts were so special, but, well, I think I need a big gulp of water. Daisy, how about coming over here and we will sit down on a firm surface for a while?"

As Grampy got some water and sat on a bench along the pier, Daisy relaxed at his feet while he stroked her head. Clayton and Austin prepared to make that special phone call. Mr. Pete prepped them on how to report the coordinates and they made a list of what relics they had seen.

"Oh, how exciting!" the lady from the Department of State said, after the boys reported their find. "My name is Melissa Price, and I will be your contact about your possible treasure. Please email to me the pictures you captured on your underwater camera. I will thoroughly search our records and will get back in touch with you young men in a day or two. I have your contact information. Thank you for notifying the State of Florida and not disturbing the underwater site."

"Wow, today is Tuesday! That means we might become rich and famous before we fly home on Saturday morning," Clayton clapped.

"Lots to do between today and Saturday," Mom advised. "You have some choices, probably can't take in everything that the Destin area has to offer by Friday night."

"Okay, let's list our choices," Austin said getting his notebook.

"The Pirate Cruise is tonight, that is a for sure thing," said Clayton's dad.

"And we get to see our fellow deckhands, Camryn and Sydney," said Clayton said, while high-fiving with Austin.

"Here are some things for you two young men to consider," Mom said.

"Number 1) a day at the beach with your buddies and fish from the beach,

Number 2) a visit to Seaside, Florida for lunch and the local bookstore, The Sundog, where you could get some advice from Miss Lainey about writing your book,

Number 3) a visit to the Indian Mounds in Fort Walton and there is another local bookstore, The Book Rack,

Number 4) a scenic trip down Hwy. 98 and Hwy. 30A to visit Rosemary Beach and Panama City Beach and all the quaint local artists' shops along the way, plus there is a small place in Grayton Beach called the Red Bar Restaurant, which is locally owned and different from any restaurant around the area.

Number 5) Gulfarium, a huge aquarium in Fort Walton.

Number 6) Fudpucker's, a restaurant with alligators,

Number 7) Destin History and Fishing Museum,

Number 8) Destin Harborwalk and A.J.'s Restaurant where you can see the charter fishing boats pull in with their daily catches, and you can even watch the anglers weigh their fish and filet them,

Are you sure you want me to keep going? Your faces are telling me you are getting overwhelmed."

"Mom, Mom, too much to think about," Clayton announced.

"I have one more option," declared Mr. Jim. "Samantha and I would enjoy taking you out on our cabin cruiser, the *African Queen*, all around Destin Harbor and we could even stop at Crabb Island for a swim. We could also go out in the Gulf and using the coordinates, 86 degrees 45'0"W latitude by 30 degrees 5'0"N longitude, obtained from the U. S. Geological Survey, we could find the DeSoto Canyon Regions. These are the 'fish havens' and also called the 'fish caverns' where the best fishing areas are located. These caverns could be as deep as 300 ft. and resemble cats' paws in their shapes."

"Wow, that brings our choices up to nine," Austin said as he scratched his head looking perplexed.

"You guys mull it over and you can search on your iPad about these places if you want. We will leave for the *Buccaneer* Pirate Cruise in one hour so you have some free time to thoughtfully consider your decisions," Mom said.

"Grampy, are you feeling better?" Mr. Pete asked.

"Much better, thanks," replied Grampy. "My head was swimming during the sub ride, and now my head is swimming from listening to all these choices of things to do and only three more days for everyone. Well, everyone except for Pete, Jim, Samantha and myself. Retirement is wonderful!"

"Don't rub it in," Mom said. "I must return to my job on Monday. And Clayton and Austin don't want to miss any school, right, boys?"

"Ha ha," Clayton answered with a grimace. "Really, though, no, I don't want to miss any school, I like the teachers and my classes."

"Me, too," Austin agreed.

While the group sat on the pier and enjoyed the beautiful scenery of Destin Harbor and continued to *ooh* and *aah* about the day's adventure in the sub, Clayton and Austin looked over the list of choices and began searching on their iPad.

"I really want to spend time with Camryn and Sydney since we are all here together. We could have lots of fun on the beach, building sand castles and making up stories plus we could use our fishing gear and even fish off the beach," said Clayton.

"Right on, buddy," said Austin. "Plus I want to stay close to our cell phones in case Miss Price calls about our treasure."

"Oh, seriously man, that is right! I want to be ready to pose for some pictures and collect some cash," Clayton laughed.

"It would be nice to talk to Miss Lainey at the Sun Dog Book Store," Austin suggested. "Maybe she could give us some hints as to how to even begin writing a book."

"A-OK with me," replied Clayton. "But look at this list, there are just too many other choices. Well...we are just going to need to make our case for returning here again. Who knows, maybe next Spring Break or next summer?"

"Awesome, yes, yes, yes," Austin chimed in.

"I vote that tomorrow we do the beach thing with our fellow-deckhands and fish from the beach, then on

Thursday, take in the Sun Dog Book Store and talk with Miss Lainey," said Clayton.

"My vote too," Austin agreed. "Maybe by Thursday afternoon, we will get that return call about our treasure, and that will determine what we do on Friday."

"First up, let's round up those pirates on the *Buccaneer*," Clayton shouted. "Onward, fellow deckhand! Let's go!"

—— Chapter 14——
Shark Sighting!

"Grampy, good morning, last night was so, SO, SO much fun," Clayton said as he pretended to sword fight with Austin.

"YES! Right on!" agreed Austin.

"And, Grampy, when you got picked for the water gun battle with Camryn and Sydney, that was hilarious," Mom added. "You got soaked."

"All in good fun, everyone, all in good fun!" Grampy added. "Even though I did get drenched. Maybe I can redeem myself today at the beach by sneaking up on Camryn and Sydney with our water guns. Clayton, may I borrow your water gun?"

"Oh, sure, it isn't anything like the huge water soaker the pirates had last night, but...it will still help you to return the favor by getting the girls really wet!"

"That means, of course, you have to provide the element of surprise to them," laughed Mom. "Hey, are you swashbucklers ready for breakfast?"

"Ready, Captain Jolly Roger Mom," answered Clayton.

"Well, I don't have a peg leg like the legendary pirate, and I am not planning to capture anyone," Mom answered, "but remember what Grampy just said about 'all in good fun' so I will laugh at that name."

As the group enjoyed their eggs, biscuits, and fruit, Grampy's cell phone rang.

"Phone, phone!" shouted Austin. "Are we rich and famous yet?"

"Okay, that sounds good, we will see you at the beach in about an hour," Grampy said as he ended the call.

"Well, was that Miss Price at the Florida State Department?" asked Clayton eagerly.

"Sorry, no. It was Austin's dad. Austin, we are meeting your mom and dad at their rental condo at Shoreline Towers on Gulf Shore Drive, one hour from now. How about you guys call Camryn and Sydney? Maybe they and their families could meet us there. I will call Jim and Samantha and Pete also."

"A-OK, will do," Clayton answered. "Everyone listen carefully for the phone today. Don't want to miss that call about our treasure."

"I will guard the phone all day, I promise," Grampy grinned.

"We are good to go," Clayton informed everyone. "Both of the girls and their families will be there at the beach."

"And Jim, Samantha, and Pete will be there too," said Grampy.

As the morning progressed, the youngsters were enjoying the nice warm weather and playing around in the ocean.

"Look over there." Camryn pointed out the remains of a shoe, a huge one, that washed up on the beach.

"That is a man's shoe," Sydney added. "Is that a bite mark in the toe part?"

"Who knows where this came from, maybe an island in the Caribbean, a ship in the Atlantic, or could be just someone who lives on a yacht and the shoe washed overboard," Austin said.

"Well...we could make up some fantastic adventure about this shoe for another chapter in our book, Austin. What do you think?"

"Since it is a stylish leather shoe, not an athletic shoe," replied Austin, "this man probably had money to afford expensive footwear. So...let's say the owner of this shoe was on an expensive yacht."

"Okay, so how did he lose the shoe?" Camryn asked.

"Maybe, just maybe, he and his wife were having a party on their anchored yacht, and everyone decided to swim. So, they all took off their shoes and dove in the water," offered Sydney.

"Well, sounds cool, but that still doesn't explain how his shoe would have fallen overboard," Clayton said, scratching his head in deep thought.

"I know, I got this!" Austin shouted. "A gang of pirates, in their old dilapidated fishing vessel, ventured close, climbed onboard the yacht, and attempted to rob the partyers as they were boarding the yacht from their swim. In the melee, our guy's shoe got pushed overboard. Any other thoughts, fellow deckhands?"

"And about that time, a U. S. Coast Guard ship pulled up, and saved the day for the yacht passengers," answered Sydney.

"And the Coast Guard personnel hauled the pirates off to the jail located in the bottom deck of the U. S. ship, and transported them to the local Coast Guard station," Clayton said as he knuckle-bumped with Austin.

"And the yacht passengers lived happily ever after. Case closed. Story finished," Camryn declared. "Of course, our yacht man had to buy another pair of leather shoes when they docked, and went shopping in town."

Everyone was laughing as the adults had overheard the kids' chatter about the adventure of the shoe.

"Thanks for using your creative juices, Sydney and Camryn, to help Austin and me with ideas for our adventure book. Of course, we could all make more contributions to the book and then we would all be the authors. We still have a few days before we all head back for home. We could work on it tomorrow afternoon after we see Miss Lainey at Seaside." Clayton offered. "Hey, by the way, is anyone other than me getting hungry?"

"Yes!" replied Austin, Camryn, and Sydney.

"We get the hint," Grampy answered. "Anyone want pizza? We could walk up the street to the Mellow Mushroom. Then we could get our fishing gear and fish from here at the beach."

"Great idea," answered Clayton.

Lunch was enjoyed by all, the fishing gear and bait were collected, and the group headed back to the beach.

"Mr. Jim, have you ever seen any sharks in the waters here?" Clayton asked. "I was just asking because the thought just hit me about adding a part to our shoe story. Maybe our yacht man got scratched during the confrontation with the pirates and there was blood on the shoe when it went over the railing. The blood was enticing to a shark and the shark tried to bite into it, thinking it was food."

"Wow, those creative juices are still flowing," Austin commented. "Good idea."

"Yes, to answer your question, there have been reported shark sightings plus some actual shark bites this year all along the coastlines of the Gulf and Atlantic. Ocean-goers have to be alert and on guard all the time."

"We have been watching the water closely and we don't walk out very far," Camryn advised.

"Great, you young ladies and gentlemen ready to cast out?" Grampy asked as he began handing out fishing rods and bait.

"Ready, set, fish!" exclaimed Clayton.

As nothing was happening on the ends of the fishing lines for what seemed like two or three hours, Grampy offered to watch the lines so the kids could dig in the sand and build a sand castle.

"Let's build a moat around our castle," suggested Sydney after the completion of the walls and windows.

"And we could design a drawbridge, too," said Austin.

"Someone's line is moving, big time!" yelled Grampy.

"Oh, that's mine," boasted Camryn. "What do I do next?"

"Let's reel it in, whatever it is!" Mom responded.

As Camryn and Mom worked and worked to bring in the catch, the spectators along the beach started gathering around them, shouting encouragement. Camryn's grandpa helped by holding tight to the end of the fishing rod that was under Camryn's right arm.

"You can do it, young lady! Keep working at it!" encouraged Mr. Pete.

"There it is!" yelled Mom. "What is it?"

"Clayton, you just asked me earlier about sharks in these waters, well...now you and your buddies can say you have officially sighted a shark," Mr. Jim said.

"SHARK! WHAT? THAT'S A SHARK?" screamed Camryn.

"SHARK SIGHTING!" shouted the spectators who had gathered.

"Yes, young lady, you have snared a baby shark," Mrs. Samantha calmly answered. "Let's take some pictures quickly, and then we can release it back into the Gulf."

"Will it bite us?" Camryn asked with a scared sounding voice.

"It is possible. Baby sharks do have teeth. So did you get your pictures, Samantha?" Mr. Jim asked.

"Got several, Jim, so everyone take a good look at the little baby and then back in the water it goes."

"We don't want the little thing to suffer any longer. I'm cutting the fishing line and sending it back on its merry way into the Gulf waters," Mr. Pete said.

"Sharks generally lose lots of teeth in their lifetime, maybe even thousands, said Mr. Jim. You might even find shark teeth on the beaches here. The town of Venice, Florida calls itself the 'shark tooth capital of the world.'"

Mrs. Samantha forwarded the shark pictures from her phone to everyone, and life seemed to return to normal.

"Enough excitement for a day," Clayton said as the kids went about finishing their sand creation and playing like pirates along the beach. The adults cleared away the fishing gear and resumed their relaxing and reading.

The sun was moving across the sky and soon it would be dark. Everyone watched the sunset over the Gulf, and Mrs. Samantha took some pictures.

"I'll forward these to everyone later," she said. "Let's get some dinner now."

"I really like Callahan's Restaurant just across the street," Mr. Pete suggested.

"Okay, let's all get cleaned up, and we will meet over there in 45 minutes," Mom said.

"Do they have cheeseburgers?" Clayton asked, and everyone laughed heartily.

"What? What's so funny?" Clayton inquired.

"Somehow we just figured that is what you would want," Mom answered.

"As long as they have cheeseburgers with bun tops, I am good!" Clayton replied. "Now in case you don't know the story behind that comment, well...I'll be glad to explain later over dinner."

—— Chapter 15 ——
Treasure – For Real!

"Really enjoyed Callahan's Restaurant last night," Camryn said, as she, Sydney, Clayton, Austin, Grampy and Mr. Jim drove down beautiful Hwy. 30A to the Red Bar Restaurant in Grayton Beach for lunch.

"And I loved your story, Clayton, about ordering a burger at the restaurant in Newport, Kentucky, and it had no top," commented Sydney.

"That was the style there," Clayton replied, laughing. "It was a place modeled after an old German restaurant."

"Yes, that was funny," Austin chimed in. "If we write a book about the adventures of Clayton and Austin, we just have to include that tale."

"So are you going to order a burger?" asked Mr. Jim, heading into the Red Bar Restaurant parking lot.

"Absolutely," answered Clayton.

"I have always enjoyed the food here," said Mr. Jim. "By the way, you will notice when you enter the restaurant that they have lots of posters on the walls and ceiling. They even have one of Elvis along with posters of other famous singers and groups. Some posters are autographed."

The group entered the restaurant and Camryn and Sydney immediately eyed a poster of Nick Jonas.

"Look! Over there! Nick Jonas! Well, it's his poster, not really him. Too bad," Camryn said, shaking her head. "Mr. Jim, do you think we could sit in that empty booth by the poster?"

Mr. Jim and Grampy asked the hostess if they all could sit there, explaining they had two awe-struck young ladies who wanted to admire Nick Jonas while they ate. The hostess proceeded to lead them to that booth.

"Thanks, Mr. Jim, thanks, Grampy, for asking for us," giggled Sydney, as she and Camryn could barely control their singing a Jonas tune long enough to look at the menu.

Everyone except Clayton ordered fish sandwiches and lunch was enjoyed by all.

"Time to head down 30A to Seaside," Mr. Jim said as the group climbed into his SUV. "Seaside has such beautiful and exquisite homes sitting among the native environment. Lots of restrictions about building there and you can't have a yard full of regular grass. You must use the natural vegetation for the area."

"Wow, that is really cool!" said Camryn. "Such an environmentally friendly town."

"Here we are, you young authors," Grampy said as Mr. Jim pulled his SUV into the parking lot at Sundog Books. "Let's go talk to Lainey about your book ideas,"

"Yeah! This is exciting," exclaimed Austin. "We have some ideas and questions for her."

After Mr. Jim introduced the four youngsters to Miss Lainey, they began discussing favorite books and authors, along with their ideas and questions about writing books.

"My advice to you is to decide what type of book you want to write," Miss Lainey began. "I wouldn't suggest trying to write two books at once. Make a decision on the fiction story named the 'Monster from the Green Trail' or the nonfiction story based on your houseboat trips, 'The Adventures of Clayton and Austin.' When you finish one story, then work on the other. Another issue for you is to decide who is your target audience? Do you plan to write for young readers and make it a picture book with few words and lots of pictures? Or, will you be writing a chapter book for your own peer group? For me, writing a picture book with young readers in mind is harder, because it is necessary to use limited vocabulary. Writing a chapter book for your age group is more freeing because you can use a wider variety of words and write similarly to the way you actually interact with others. The last piece of advice is to make the cover dramatic with the characters' eyes drawing a reader into the story."

"Wow, thanks Miss Lainey," Clayton said. "We will have a lot to discuss on our ride back to Destin."

"Oh, I enjoy talking to such motivated young people," Miss Lainey answered. "And don't forget to look over what you write, and REVISE, REVISE, REVISE! Good authors revise multiple times."

After Clayton, Austin, Sydney and Camryn each purchased a book, the group said their good-byes. During the ride home, the kids made the decision to write the fictional story about the green trail monster first.

"Too bad we don't all live in the same city," commented Austin, "but we still have tomorrow to work on this story. And then, we all fly out on Saturday and back to our homes."

"We will be able to call or email to make book decisions," Clayton suggested.

Just then, their deep conversation and thoughts were interrupted with the sound of Grampy's cell phone ringing.

"Maybe it is Miss Price about our TREASURE!" an excited Austin said.

The youngsters kept their eyes and ears glued to Grampy until he concluded his conversation.

"Well, are we rich and famous?" Clayton asked with hesitation.

"Not yet, guys," answered Grampy. "Miss Price said the site that you found was already listed in the Florida Master File Site, but they will send an underwater crew to further investigate the site. She commented it was so helpful that you included the marine coordinates for the site. The State of Florida will send each of you young gentlemen a certificate thanking you for notifying them about the find. They will also communicate further with you if they find anything new at the site."

"Sorry, Clayton and Austin, that's a bummer," consoled Sydney.

"No kidding," Clayton replied as he and Austin looked at each other with dejected faces.

"You know what, guys?" Grampy smiled. "You maybe didn't find any new shipwreck site with millions of dollars' worth of Spanish coins, but...think about it, you four kiddos are planning to write a book, maybe even two books. Books are like 'treasure' because you help others to enjoy and share literature, plus you get to enjoy creating something all your own. So...books are like 'treasure' to the readers and authors."

"Good idea, Grampy," said Camryn.

"So be proud of yourselves!" said Mr. Jim. "Here we are, back at Shoreline Towers. Do you young folks want to play around on the beach this afternoon?"

"Awesome!" shouted Clayton as the kids exited the car. "Austin and I could meet you back on the beach here when? How about in 20 minutes?"

"Sounds good," said Camryn.

"I'll be there," agreed Sydney.

The group enjoyed another afternoon on the beach and were getting ready to head in to change clothes and go to dinner at McGuire's Irish Restaurant.

"Wait!" shouted Clayton, "I see something sparkly. It's sticking out of the sand. Come over here and look!"

"Sure you aren't taking up your Grampy's way of joking around?" Sydney questioned.

"NO WAY!" Clayton replied. "Let's dig!"

"It's a bracelet, looks like diamonds," Camryn commented, her eyes getting big like saucers. "Hey, it might be made of REAL diamonds, not fake. TREASURE!"

"Since this is the beach for Shoreline Towers, let's take it to the office and see if anyone there lost it," Austin suggested.

After packing up their belongings and the newly found bracelet, the youngsters walked to the office explaining how they found their new 'treasure.'

"Oh my! One of our residents, Sara Morgan Lose, was in here just about 10 minutes ago. She lost her diamond bracelet and this one looks just like the bracelet she described," Miss Sharon told them. "I will call her and ask her to come to the office."

"Oh, that is it! My husband gave it to me for my birthday," Miss Sara exclaimed when she walked into the office. "Thank you, thank you."

"You're welcome," all the young people replied.

"I want to give you nice young people something as a reward. I need to go to my condo, and I'll be back in just a minute," Miss Sara answered as she ran to the elevator.

Clayton, Austin, Sydney and Camryn just stared at each other with perplexed faces.

"Here you go," Miss Sara said with a shiver in her voice as she stepped off the elevator. She handed each of them a $50 bill. "I am so happy you found my bracelet. It is a real TREASURE to me."

After the thank yous were exchanged all around, the kids went to Mr. Jim and Mrs. Samantha's condo to join up with the adults. They relayed their story of the recovered bracelet and the reward money they received.

"Great news," Grampy declared. "Your bonus of $50 each is very special. So proud of you all for being good citizens."

"Guess what she told us?" said Clayton. "She told us the bracelet was real TREASURE to her. And she was so excited that she even had tears in her eyes."

"So being able to give her so much happiness was something that gave you a lot of happiness too, right?" asked Mom.

"Oh yes, I got tears in my eyes too," Camryn said.

The group then decided to spend the next day visiting Miss Melli at the Book Rack in Fort Walton Beach to get her advice on selling books and then spend the afternoon on the beach before returning to their homes on Saturday.

"Before we go to dinner, I have an important announcement," Grampy said, looking unusually serious. "After numerous discussions with Clayton's Mom and Dad, I have decided to make my permanent home aboard the *Granny Rose* here in Destin. I will be renting the boat slip next to Jim and Samantha's cruiser at the Destin Plantation Marina. I plan to put my house in Louisville, along with my pickup truck, up for sale and purchase another vehicle here. Clayton, Austin, and my daughter and son-in-law, I know I will miss you but I have a bunch of friends in the Panhandle area to keep me occupied. Plus, Camryn, your Grandma Lilly and Grandpa Logan will be wintering over here in Destin."

"Grampy, I...I don't know...well...I'm not sure what to say," Clayton rambled. "Will definitely miss you."

"Same here," said Austin.

"Now you know, listen up everyone here, I will gladly welcome visits from you anytime!" Grampy said with an unusually straight face which turned into a wide grin. "And I am NOT joking!"

"We have learned and seen so much on this trip, Grampy, thanks," Clayton said. You are a TREASURE TO US! TREASURE - FOR REAL!"

As Clayton, Austin, Camryn and Sydney surrounded Grampy and bear-hugged him, all the adults congratulated Grampy on his decision.

"I was thinking about for one month next summer." Grampy advised. "If any of you four deckhands or any of you adults want to join me on another houseboat cruise further east on the Intracoastal Waterway, I would love the company! Won't make the whole Big C in one month obviously, but we could probably make it to southern Florida and maybe up the Eastern Seaboard a little. My target is completing a trip to Daytona Beach."

"DID YOU HEAR THAT?" Clayton said loud enough for all to hear. MORE ADVENTURES TO COME!

Nautical Language

Aft
The back section of a vessel.

Bow
The front side of a vessel.

Bridge
The place in the vessel where the controls are located.
(Example - steering wheel, gears, etc.)

Captain
First person in command of a vessel.

Channel
That part of a waterway open to navigation.

Coordinates
A system used in geography enabling every location on Earth to be specified by a set of numbers, letters, or symbols.

Deckhand
Helper on a vessel.

Depth gauge
Measures the distance from bottom of vessel to bottom of waterway.

First mate

Second person in command of a vessel - takes captain's place if necessary.

Flatboat

A boat with about 2 – 3 ft. sides all around, no point in front, with a flat bottom.

Knot

A unit of speed equal to one international nautical mile per hour, exactly 1.852 kilometers per hour (approximately 1.15078 miles per hour).

Latitude

A measurement on a globe or map of location north or south of Equator.

Longitude

A measurement east or west of the prime meridian at Greenwich, London, the specifically designated imaginary north – south line that passes through both geographical poles and Greenwich.

Moorings

Ropes and any attachments that connect a vessel to a dock.

Mouth

Point where one waterway drains into another waterway.

Port
Left side of a vessel.

Starboard
Right side of a vessel.

Stern
Rear of a vessel.

Vessel
Any size watercraft.

Wake
Waves given off by the movement of a vessel.

Wheelhouse
Area of vessel that contains the steering controls and gauges.

Special Resources for Parents, Grandparents and Teachers

(based on <u>Clayton's Intracoastal Waterway Adventure</u> by Linda M. Penn and Frank J. Feger)

Before the reading:

1. Recall when you were in a crowd of people. How did the tight space make you feel?

2. Do you have any family members who are in the United States military – Army, Navy, Air Force, Coast Guard, or Marines?

3. Have you ever seen an alligator, stingray, or shark? Were you scared?

4. Tell about anything unusual you have found when digging in sand or dirt.

5. Would you want to fly a plane? Why or why not?

6. Describe any experiences you have had while riding in a boat.

7. Would you like to ride in a submarine? Explain.

During the Reading:

1. How did Clayton, Austin, Grampy, Mom, and Daisy react when they saw the *Granny Rose* again? (Chapter 1)

2. How did the City of Mobile get its name? (Chapter 2)

3. Explain why Clayton said that the USS Alabama was like a monster. (Chapter 3)

4. Why did the crew of a battleship clean the decks every day? (Chapter 3)

5. Why do you think Grampy looked over the Departure List before leaving the dock and guiding the boat in the water? (Chapter 4)

6. What did Clayton think he saw in Mobile Bay? (Chapter 4)

7. Why do you think the early inhabitants of Dauphin Island allowed the animals to roam free? Chapter 4)

8. Why did goats climb trees on Dauphin Island? (Chapter 5)

9. In your opinion, why did the Sea Lab workers tell visitors to use two fingers to pet the stingrays? (Chapter 6)

10. Describe the environment at the Bird Sanctuary. (Chapter 6)

11. Tell about Grampy and Mom's favorite places on Dauphin Island. (Chapter 7)

12. How do professional fishermen know about the best places to fish? (Chapter 7)

13. Why did Austin blow the foghorn? (Chapter 8)

14. Name some characteristics of the Intracoastal Waterway? (Chapter 9)

15. Why was Austin confused about his career plans? (Chapter 9)

16. Who was "Sneaky Pete" and why do you think he was given this nickname? (Chapter 10)

17. What could be the reasons Daisy barked whenever the periscope was in sight? (Chapters 11 and 12)

18. Summarize Mr. Pete's tour of duty on a U.S. Navy submarine and explain why he bought a yellow submarine. (Chapter 12)

19. What did Clayton and Austin's research tell about the recovery of treasure from shipwrecks? (Chapters 12 and 13)

20. Describe Clayton, Austin, Camryn and Sydney's "shoe adventure." (Chapter 14)

21. Why do you think Miss Lainey suggested working on only one book at a time? (Chapter 15)

22. How did Miss Sara feel about the boys and girls finding her lost bracelet? (Chapter 15)

23. What were Grampy's plans for himself and the *Granny Rose*? (Chapter 15)

After the Reading:

1. Evaluate the kids' decision to write a book.

2. What actions of the kids show their continuing maturity?

3. Will Grampy enjoy living in Destin? Explain your answer.

Social Studies, Science, Technology, Math, and Writing Project

Your town is receiving more and more visitors because of the recently opened "Adventure Park," a destination with hiking trails, rafting, fishing, playground, picnic area, and classes about nature preservation. At last night's City Council meeting, the City Commissioners discussed purchasing property adjoining the park and expanding the picnic area to have a shelter with meeting rooms for the classes, and new restrooms.

Research about the economic and environmental pros and cons for your town.

Provide a written report and oral presentation for the next City Council meeting.

References

Abramson, Andrea Serlin. *Submarines Up Close*. New York, New York: Sterling Publishing Co., Inc., 2007.

uss.alabama.com

Appleton, Victor (pseud.). *Tom Swift and His Submarine Boat, or Under the Ocean For Sunken Treasure*. A Public Domain Book.

beachchairscientist.com

blueangels.navy.mil

Brown, Jeff and Houran Haskins, Lori. *Flat Stanley and the Lost Treasure*. New York, New York: Harper Collins Publishers, 2016.

captainjohn.org

charterfishingdestin.com

coastalbirding.org

curiouscraig.net/2018/03/03battleship-park-mobile-al

Dauphin Island Life Magazine, Mobile, Alabama: Discover Gulf Coast Alabama, 2018.

destinfishingrodeo.org

destinlog.com

Dillon, Sharon. (2016, January, 17). Personal interview.

disl.org/estuarium

dos.myflorida.com/historical/about/division-faqs/underwater-archeology

explainthatstuff.com/submarines

Federspiel, Donna. (2018, May, 12). Personal interview.

foxnews.com/science/2018/07/12/16th-century-shipwreck-off-florida-coast-is-worth-millions.html

globalsubdive.com/submarine-or-submersible-whats-the-difference/

GPS-coordinates.org

healthline.com. Scaccia, Annamarya. "*Everything You Should Know About Claustrophobia,*" November 29, 2016.

history.navy.mil

learner.org

livescience.com/55793-photos-colonial-age-shipwrecks-cape-canaveral.html

militaryfactory.com/ships/detail.asp?ship-id=USS-Drum-SS228

navalaviationmuseum.org

Penn, Gilbert. (2018, March, 3). Personal interview.

pirates.wikia.com

planetscience.com/humanbodyfearof heights

seamagine.com/expedition-submarine-6-person.html

sedwickcoins.com

Shellinbarger, Deanne. Shellinbarger.Scott. (2018, January, 23). Personal interview.

smithsonianmag.com

Thomas, Paul. (2018, April, 30). Personal interview.

throwedrolls.com

tritonsubs.com

Uithoven, Carroll. *Dauphin Island, Alabama.* Cedar Rapids, Iowa: WDG Publishing, 2014.

Vesilind, Priit J. *Lost Gold of the Republic.* Las Vegas, Nevada: Shipwreck Heritage Press, 2005.

Visit Mobile Magazine. Gulf Shores, Alabama: Compass Media, Inc., 2016.

walrus.wr.usgs.gov/pacmaps/ds-nebt.html

Warfel, Julia. (2018, March, 4). Personal interview.

Watanabe, Janice (2018, March, 19). Personal interview.

weather.com, "*Michael Unearths 19th Century Ships Wrecked on Florida's Dog Island During 1899 Hurricane,*" October 22, 2018.

Wikipedia>wiki>Destin-Florida

Wikipedia>wiki>Eglin-Air-Force-Base

Wikipedia>wiki>Intracoastal-Waterway

Clayton's Fast Facts About the Intracoastal Waterway

❀ The Intracoastal Waterway is a 3,000 mile inland waterway along the Atlantic Ocean and Gulf of Mexico coasts of the United States.

❀ It runs from Boston, Massachusetts, southward, along the Atlantic Seaboard and around the southern tip of Florida, then following the Gulf Coast to Brownsville, Texas.

❀ Sections of the waterway consist of natural inlets, rivers, bays, and sounds, while others are artificial canals.

❀ It was opened in 1912 to improve transportation routes for all geographic regions.

❀ The U.S. Army Corps of Engineers has responsibility for waterway improvements and maintenance.

❀ The waterway is used by barges, recreational boaters, and by ocean-going boaters who find the ocean too rough for travel.

About the Author
Linda M. Penn

Linda M. Penn holds a master's degree and Rank I degree in Elementary Education from the University of Louisville. She taught kindergarten thru third grade for 21 years in public schools.

Since retirement, Linda has been writing children's books, and presenting at writing conferences, schools and libraries.

Her books include: Is Kentucky in the Sky; Hunter and the Fast Car Trophy Race; The Avenue; Clayton's Birding Adventure; No More French Fries in the Bed; No Pink Glasses. All of these books are picture books for ages 3 - 6.

Linda has written four children's chapter books with her cousin, Frank J. Feger, Clayton's River Adventure; Clayton's River Adventure Continues: Cincinnati to Frankfort; Clayton's River Adventure Frankfort to Boonesborough; and the latest book, Clayton's River Adventure Louisville to Paducah. These books are for ages 7-11. Linda and Frank are working on more books in the Clayton series.

Linda's website and blog, lindampenn.com, has many resources for parents and teachers to enhance the reading experience with their young ones. These resources can be downloaded for free.

You can contact her at lindampenn@gmail.com.

About the Author
Frank J. Feger

Frank was born in Louisville, KY, graduated from St. Xavier High School and United Electronics Institute. He served three years in the U.S. Army.

Frank was a Medical Electronics Sale Representative for 40 years, having worked for Malkin Instrument Co. and sold pacemakers, defibrillators and cardiac monitors for 10 years. He worked for Olympus Medical Corp. for 30 years and sold gastrointestinal endoscopes in Kentucky, Indiana and Ohio. Frank retired in 2007 and is the VP for the Colon Cancer Prevention Project in Louisville, KY.

Frank has been a boater for 56 years. The boat mentioned in the book, the *Granny Rose*, was a 42-foot Harbor Master houseboat that made two trips to Cincinnati. Frank and his family enjoyed the boat and the trips all his family and friends embarked on.

At a family reunion, Linda and Frank met upon an interesting boating conversation. Linda had already been thinking about publishing another Clayton book, and upon hearing Frank's river traveling stories, the two decided to mesh their experiences together and embark on another Clayton adventure – this time down the Ohio and Kentucky Rivers.

About the Illustrator
Melissa Quinio

Melissa Noel Quinio went to the University of Louisville to study Fine Arts and Psychology. She now lives in Lexington, Kentucky with her four children (two boys and two girls) and her husband, Edward. She spends her time creating new and exciting works of art and spending precious time with her family.

CPSIA information can be obtained
at www.ICGtesting.com
Printed in the USA
FSHW011116260519